Meyers'
Rebellion

BY CONNIE BRUMMEL CROOK

Fitzhenry & Whiteside

Published in Canada by Fitzhenry & Whiteside,
195 Allstate Parkway, Markham, Ontario L3R 4T8

Published in the United States by Fitzhenry & Whiteside,
311 Washington Street, Brighton, Massachusetts 02135

www.fitzhenry.ca   godwit@fitzhenry.ca

10 9 8 7 6 5 4 3 2 1

Library and Archives Canada Cataloguing in Publication

Crook, Connie Brummel
Meyers' rebellion / Connie Brummel Crook.

ISBN 1-55041-943-9

1. Canada—History—Rebellion, 1837-1838—Juvenile fiction.
2. United Empire loyalists—Juvenile fiction. I. Title.

PS8555.R6113M493 2005   jC813'.54   C2005-903643-5

U.S. Publisher Cataloging-in-Publication Data
(Library of Congress Standards)

Crook, Connie Brummel
Meyers' rebellion / Connie Brummel Crook
[246] p. ; cm.
Summary: The humorous story of a boy's exploits during the Upper Canada Rebellion
The third in the saga of the Meyers family, Loyalists and early Canadian settlers.
ISBN 1-55041-943-9
1. Canada — History — Rebellion, 1837-1838 — Fiction. 2. Frontier and pioneer life —
Ontario — Fiction. I. Title.
813/.54 [Fic] 22   PZ7.C8818Me 2005

Fitzhenry & Whiteside acknowledges with thanks the Canada Council for the Arts,
and the Ontario Arts Council for their support of our publishing program.
We acknowledge the financial support of the Government of Canada through the Book
Publishing Industry Development Program (BPIDP) for our publishing activities.

Canada Council   Conseil des Arts
for the Arts   du Canada

ONTARIO ARTS COUNCIL
CONSEIL DES ARTS DE L'ONTARIO

Design by Wycliffe Smith Design Inc.
Cover illustration by David Craig

Printed in Canada

OTHER BOOKS BY CONNIE BRUMMEL CROOK

NOVELS

The Meyers Saga
Flight
Meyers' Creek

The Nellie McClung trilogy
Nellie L.
Nellie's Quest
Nellie's Victory

The Story of Laura Secord
Laura's Choice

Historical Years in Upper Canada
The Hungry Year
The Perilous Year

PICTURE BOOKS
Maple Moon
Laura Secord's Brave Walk
Lune d'érable

DEDICATION

To my two fine sons-in-law:
Marc Beranger, who has been my technical adviser
from the start and a wonderful Web master,
and
Dan Floyd, who critiques and also assists
in writing descriptions of sports events for my stories.
Thank you both for all the time and patience.

ACKNOWLEDGEMENTS

Many thanks to all the people, experts and fellow amateurs both, who have helped in the preparation of this book. If any errors remain, they are mine, not theirs. In particular, I would like to thank:

- Mary Beacock Fryer for her many wonderful historical books, especially *A Military History of the Rebellions of Upper Canada: Volunteers & Redcoats* and *Rebels & Raiders*, which helped to clarify this time of our rebellions. I admire greatly her many historical accounts that bring so much of Canada's history to life.

- Betsy Dewar Boyce of Belleville, Ontario, for her very interesting, informative, well-researched and documented book *The Rebels of Hastings* (University of Toronto Press).

- My sister Eleanor and her husband Robert Bruce of Belleville, Ontario, who guided my research of the rough northern route around Bon Echo Park, where Bob, an O.P.P. officer, had participated in search and rescue operations.

- David Rumball of Peterborough, Ontario, for researching for me at the Archives of Ontario in Toronto.

- James Kimber, a Peterborough neighbour, who gave me very old maps and books from his Toronto ancestors' attic.

- Edwin Crook, my brother-in-law from Letellier, Manitoba, for research about beverages at Montgomery's Tavern.

- My cousins, Thornton and Doris Brummel of Napanee, Ontario, for their research and answers to questions about the Napanee area, where they have lived most of their lives.
- Mrs. Mildred Sussell of Jackson, Michigan, a Meyers descendant, for her detailed genealogical research.
- Mr. Doug Knutson of Belleville, Ontario, producer of the documentary about John W. Meyers, who has answered many questions pertaining to my ancestors, the Meyers, and their descendants.
- Colleen Allen and other helpful librarians in the Reference Department of Peterborough Public Library.
- Professor Kirk A.Whipper, C.M., O.Ont., M.A., M.Ed., D.Mus., for advice on canoes. How I have enjoyed his very interesting and informative seminars on canoes and our history at the Canadian Canoe Museum in Peterborough, Ontario.
- Lawyer and writer Mr. Peter B. Lillico, of Peterborough, Ontario, who reviewed my legal chapter about the case taken in July 1838 by the young lawyer, John A.Macdonald. His detailed corrections and advice are greatly valued.
- Laura Peetoom for most helpful suggestions and editing, and Gail Winskill of Fitzhenry & Whiteside for encouragement.

PROLOGUE

We are not now that strength which in old days
Moved earth and heaven; that which we are, we are;
One equal temper of heroic hearts,
Made weak by time and fate, but strong in will
To strive, to seek, to find, and not to yield.
Alfred, Lord Tennyson

"You're a fool, Jacob. If it weren't for the British, we'd be nowhere!"

John W. Meyers thrust his hands deep into the pockets of his twill pants and strode over to the window. The old military man looked down proudly at the mill he'd built on the east side of the Moira River just north of his house in Belleville. He'd built the place himself with bricks he'd made on a back lot in Thurlow Township. Now, everyone from miles around came to his mill—including his youngest son, Jacob, who'd hauled twelve sacks of wheat in from his farm in Sydney Township that morning.

"We'd be nowhere?" said Jacob, thumping a mug of hot cider down on the oak table. Outside, the autumn winds were whistling through the brittle leaves on the oaks that stood guard around Meyers' two-storey brick home. "If the British had handled things properly, the Americans would never have rebelled, and we'd still be living peacefully south of the border!"

"But you wouldn't have been given a 200-acre farm as a gift from the British government if it weren't for that revolution!" Meyers pointed out, running his hands through his white curly hair with satisfaction.

"A gift?" said Jacob. "It's the least the British owed you after the risks you took on their behalf! And only half of my farm came from them, anyway. I paid for the other half through my own hard work!" Jacob was forty-five now, with seven children of his own. It was about time his father gave him some credit.

"Any man worth his salt is willing to work!" Meyers shot back, his lively grey-green eyes snapping. "And the British are the ones to work for. Stay true to them, my son."

"Until when? It's 1821 now. We've all been working hard for years, and what do we get? Bishop Strachan!"

"Strachan is a good friend of mine."

"Well, he's no friend of mine—or of any other farmer! He and the Parliament in York are playing favourites. If you're not Church of England or a recent British immigrant, you're not worth much in their sight! If someone doesn't put a stop to it, we'll have one class of people lording it over the rest. Do you want that in Upper Canada?"

"Befriend all men, Jacob, but act wisely." Then Meyers laughed as he added, "And make sure you're in the top class!"

Jacob shook his head and drained the last of his cider. "Well, Father, I need to start loading up," he said.

"What's your rush? The day's fine," said Meyers. "Sky's as clear as a bell, and that's pretty good for the eighteenth of November."

Jacob shrugged. "That's just it. We haven't had a big storm yet, and that makes me uneasy."

"Get going, then, if you need to, and remember me to Jane and the children."

Meyers watched his son head down the steep slope to the mill. Yes, he was proud of his family and he knew he should be content. But a great restlessness still came over him at times. There must be one more mountain to climb, one more task to complete…which reminded him: two of his grandsons were supposed to be completing a job at the mill. Meyers had meant to check on them an hour ago. They were probably just loafing around this very minute. Young men these days had no idea what real work was!

Meyers took his leather coat off the hook by the door and swung it over his shoulder. No need to wrap up on such a fine day, he thought. He went out the door and strode down the hill.

"Meyers!" A man with a weatherbeaten face stepped out from behind the oak trees and stood in front of him.

"Showdea," Meyers exclaimed. "It's good to see you!" His

Mississauga friend had helped Meyers build his mill, and one autumn many years ago, they had gone hunting together. Meyers had saved Showdea from a black bear.

"I haven't seen you for months!" said Meyers. "Come up to the house. I've got hot apple cider on the hob."

Showdea looked down towards the mill and the water. His eyes were bright and clear, and his grey-black hair was drawn back in a long ponytail. His buckskin jacket was brightly decorated with red beads on the pockets. Showdea seemed to be staring at something far away.

Showdea shook his head. "I'm here for a reason," he said. "You saved my life many years ago, and I want to repay you."

"There's no need, Showdea. I thank God we both got out alive."

"I, too, thank the Creator that I have lived to be an old man."

An old man? Meyers was startled. Showdea was only a few years older than Meyers himself, wasn't he? And even though he was seventy-seven, Meyers was well able to do a full day's work.

"I also want to thank you—while I can." Showdea looked steadily at his friend of so many years. Like Meyers, the Missisauga had young, lively eyes, but his head was bowed and his voice was not strong. He, too, had spent most of his days in hard work.

Meyers clapped Showdea on the shoulder. "All right, then…what did you have in mind?"

"I'd like to show you the way to the Silver Cave," Showdea said.

"The Silver Cave?" Meyers' face lit up and he raised his eyebrows. "Few Mississaugas know the way to the Silver Cave, Showdea, and none has ever told a white man." Meyers looked uncomfortable. "Are you sure?"

Showdea understood. "It is a closely guarded secret, yes— but you I can trust not to take much more than you might need." The man's voice was calm and steady.

Meyers chuckled. He'd show his children and grandchildren and all the people in Belleville that he wasn't an old man yet. One more adventure to top all his others!

Showdea had provisions enough for them both. Soon they were making their way through the black waters of the Moira River in Showdea's canoe, made of sheets of birchbark over white cedar planking, swift and strong. The two men's paddles broke the water with strong, deep strokes. They sped ahead in silence, each one lost in his own thoughts.

The fast-moving canoe gave Meyers a thrill he had not felt in months. Wind and spray flew against his cheeks, bringing back memories of the war days when he'd raced down the Hudson River pursued by American rebel forces. He laughed and pulled his paddle even harder, to match his companion's strokes.

They had not gone far when black clouds covered the sun and the landscape darkened. So Jacob had been right. Meyers shivered in spite of himself.

"That's a snow storm blowing up in the west," Showdea shouted over his shoulder. "We'll have to outrun it. Let's head for the bank—to the right."

Meyers hardly had time to pull back on his paddle when the storm hit with a sudden fury. The air filled with wind-driven snow and Meyers and Showdea were caught in an inferno of icy spray. Showdea shouted something through the blinding whiteness, but Meyers could not hear him—and in the next instant, a standing wave swamped the canoe.

The canoe rolled sideways and then capsized. Meyers was thrown face down in the icy waters. He gasped for breath as the shock of the cold went straight through to his skin. He clung to his paddle and reached for the canoe, but it was bouncing beyond him. Better to make for the nearest bank of the river. He knew the canoe wouldn't go far before it would be washed ashore and caught on one of the sharp corners. The Moira was a winding river with many ledges and rapids that would tend to work in their favour.

Meyers flailed around, the paddle still in his right hand, but somehow kept afloat. He turned his head a bit to look for his friend. "Showdea?" he shouted.

"You all right?" came a voice from the deeper water behind him.

"Great," Meyers said through clenched teeth. "Beat you to the bank." He set out for the edge of the water but found out he wasn't the fast swimmer he used to be—not in this cold water, anyway.

Even before Meyers reached the stony bank, the waves grew lighter and the snow squall began to end. He caught hold of an overhanging branch and pulled himself onto the bank. He'd beat Showdea, he thought, with the enthusiasm of a boy as he climbed out and sank to the ground. Showdea came right behind him.

"A great adventure!" Meyers smiled between coughs. "Let's go back home and start out again tomorrow!"

"No," said Showdea, shivering in his buckskin. "Perhaps it is too late in the year to trust the weather—even such seasoned men as we could lose our lives."

"Spring is a long way off," said Meyers regretfully. "Is the cave much farther?"

"Yes," answered Showdea.

A silence fell between them, and Showdea began to gather small twigs for a fire. The sun came out.

"We're only a few miles from home. Come back with me and dry out," Meyers suggested.

"You go to your castle and I will stay here in mine," Showdea laughed. "But warm up a little before you go."

"I've been through worse," said Meyers. "And my skin's like leather now. I'd best be on my way."

Meyers held out a hand to his friend. Showdea walked around his little pile of twigs and clasped his companion's cold hand with his own half-frozen one.

"In the spring," he said.

"Yes, in the spring," said Meyers. Turning, he strode energetically along the path beside the Moira River. The sun shining brightly on his wet body gave him little warmth.

PART ONE

Accidental
Rebel

1

"Watch out, you're heading for another big rut!" George yelled. "What do you think you're doing?!"

"I know what I'm doing. I saw it!" John pulled back on the reins and steered Bonnie and Duke away from near-disaster. The two roan horses snorted and strained, the breath from their nostrils turning frosty in the snapping-cold air.

It was the second of December, Saturday market day in Toronto. John and his brother had come all the way from Sydenham Township, just west of Belleville—two whole days of travel. It was the most driving John had ever done. Too bad it had to be with bossy George. He had shared the driving equally, true; but when it was John's turn, George watched him like a hawk. So what if he was twenty-four years old and a lot more experienced? He wasn't in charge yet.

John sighed. That was what happened when you had four older brothers. You were criticized and teased to death. At five feet eight inches, John was tall for his fifteen years, tall enough to defend himself. But that didn't help—he was red-haired with a temper to match, and his brothers frequently got the better of his short fuse.

"Looks like we've got lots of competition," said George. It was nine in the morning and they'd arrived at the intersection of King and Lot—along with more than a dozen other farmers with carts full of turnips, apples, chickens, pears, and pigs. Most of them had come from the nearby county of Durham or from York and Simcoe to the north, and all were headed for the St. Lawrence Market, right at the shore of Toronto Bay.

They successfully dodged scores of carriages, carts, wagons, and pedestrians and finally arrived at the huge market just south of Front Street. Toronto was not the best place for the Meyerses to sell their produce. Usually they went to Belleville. But Father had heard that many people actually paid cash in Toronto, and he wanted to have a fair bit of hard currency on hand, in case the rumours of rebellion shut the banks for a while. Not everything could be obtained through barter.

John held the horses while George went over to the market to hire a stall. They'd taken the buffalo robes off, so people going by could see their wares: apples and potatoes, salt pork from two freshly slaughtered pigs, and pies and cakes that Mother had just baked. They'd been instructed to sell absolutely everything.

They got off to a good start. A woman in a full green skirt and a rose-coloured shawl stepped down from her carriage, helped by her driver. The brim of her stiff bonnet was loaded with silk flowers and her sleeves were so big they would never fit into a coat. But her waist was so tiny it seemed almost to disappear. John stared in awe. His mother and sisters didn't have waists like that! Not even Nan Burditt on the farm next door to home looked that slim.

"Let me see the side ribs!" she commanded. How could a woman with such a slight figure have a voice so big? But John got over his surprise in a hurry. He didn't want to miss a sale. In an instant, he pulled the broadcloth from the fresh meat.

"Well, it'll have to be parboiled to remove all that salt, but it looks fresh." She nodded to her driver and motioned for him to pick out a number of the chunks. He placed them in a huge basket on his left arm.

Then the well-dressed lady saw the barrels of apples, the pumpkin loaves, and the fruit cakes—and stepped around to the end of the wagon.

"Would you like to try the cake?" John attempted to sound as pleasant as possible. He cut a piece and held it out on the point of the knife. He was hoping to avoid more sales talk.

The lady's gloved fingers removed the chunk of cake, and she took a cautious bite. "It's good! I'll take all you have."

John smiled as he handed over the ten cakes. Then she spotted the pies and took six of them. And when the woman paid the full price, plus a bit extra for him to keep, he was so excited he almost dropped all the money in the mud.

As John was stashing the money in a leather pouch, George reappeared to say there were no places inside the market building. So they just kept selling right off the wagon. The customers kept coming.

"Can you believe this town, George?" said John. "Only about two hours gone, and our wagon's almost empty and we have lots of cash."

"Don't tell the world, Johnny!"

"Can we go and see the rest of the city when we've sold it all?"

"You know what Father said. We have to leave for home right away."

John looked so disappointed that George smiled and said, "I can handle things for a while. But don't be gone long."

"I'll come right back," said John.

George could be decent every so often, John thought as he weaved in and out between wagons. And if they could make this much money in a day, they'd have a great future as businessmen. John, for one, needed money. His grandfather had left a farm to each of John's brothers and sisters, but John hadn't been born yet when Grandpa Meyers had written his will.

Oh, well, who cares? thought John as he glanced at a cage full of geese and the man selling them. He had another plan. Somehow, someday, he was going to find the Silver Cave. Grandpa Meyers had died of pneumonia after looking for it in the wilderness north of Belleville. His canoe had capsized and he was so stubborn that he walked all the way home on a freezing November day. But John would be more careful than that. And he would find that cave, though many others had failed.

As John was daydreaming, the sound of bagpipes pierced the air. He looked around and realized the music—if you could call it that—was coming from the south side of the market, not far from Toronto Bay. John ran towards the sound.

Standing on the back of a wagon parked beside the market was a strangely built man, not more than five foot six, if he was even that tall. He had a large head with a high forehead, topped by an unruly mop of flaming red hair. Another man, in a raggedy coat and an old kilt, was playing the pipes beside him, his cheeks puffed out like a squirrel's.

John squeezed in closer. The man had no produce on his wagon—only a few crates filled with paper sheets. What could he be selling?

A hush fell over the few farmers gathered around.

"There is discontent, vengeance and rage in the air," the red-haired man began. "The depression that hit us in '36 has not let up. Jobs are scarce and money is scarcer. Farmers and other businessmen compete against imports—but still we have food shortages."

The man stuffed his hands in his pockets. He was wearing only a light frock coat and baggy trousers, though the air was brisk. "We've had many years of corrupt rule by the Tories and their Executive Council. It must not continue! We must *fight* for liberty!"

The farmers cheered and one of them waved his cap in the air.

"Sir Francis Bond Head was appointed as lieutenant-governor by the King to be his ears and our voice—but he hears only his own friends and relations, and speaks only for himself! He acts like he's a king—and claims we crowned him, in so-called fair elections! But do you know why his Tories now hold the Legislative Assembly? Do you know why they control all appointments to the Executive Council and the Legislative Council? Do you?"

"Why?" shouted one farmer, who was sitting on a pickle barrel off to the right. The sun was getting higher in the sky, and the speaker on the wagon squinted against the light.

"You are right to ask why, sir," he said. "And the answer is simple. It's election fraud. Yes, we Reformers brought charges against the government for election fraud, but the government would not investigate those charges—because they would have to look at themselves.

"Now ask *yourselves:* Do you want a self-appointed government and fraud at election time?"

"No!""

"Do you want an established church with ministers paid by the State?"

"No! Equality for all denominations!"

"Do you want to elect your own justices of the peace?"

"We do! We do!"

"Do you want to elect your own governors and legislative councillors?"

Cheers rose and almost drowned out the shouts of "Yes! Yes!" rising from the growing crowd. The little man smiled and, to John's surprise, grabbed his hair and tossed it in the air. It was a red wig!! He caught it and clamped it back down on his bald head.

John gaped. Now he knew who the man was—Toronto's mayor, William Lyon Mackenzie. Last year, he and his Reform Party had challenged the Tories and been defeated. Now Sir Francis Bond Head and his circle—the friends and relations Mackenzie had dubbed "the Family Compact"—controlled every aspect of government, with transplanted English nobles and such taking every position of power. Canada was rapidly becoming a country of the very rich and the very poor. But obviously, Mackenzie hadn't given up the fight. Perhaps the crates in the wagon contained free copies of his newspaper, *The Colonial Advocate.*

The crowd was growing thicker around John now. They were pushing and shoving, but John was a sturdy boy and would not be shunted aside. He stared up at Mackenzie. The man turned, and his piercing blue eyes looked straight down into John's frowning face. He smiled at the fifteen-year-old boy as if they were both party to a secret no one else knew.

"So you want us to be Yankees!" said a sarcastic voice practically in John's right ear. John glanced at the man standing beside him. The man was no farmer, that was for sure, so thin, pallid, and unhealthy-looking was he. John looked to the other side, and discovered that he was surrounded by such men, all wearing ragged pants and torn short-coats.

"No, but I would like a government more like theirs," Mackenzie snapped back in his high-pitched voice. "I admire many aspects of the American democracy."

Thummmmphk! A rotten apple landed smack in the middle of the small man's head. The crowd fell silent, but Mackenzie acted as if nothing had happened.

"Brave Canadians!" he went on. "Do you love freedom? I

know you do. Do you hate oppression? Then put down these villains who are taking over our country!"

Two men stepped forward—one a sturdy fellow with heavy side whiskers and unruly hair; the other a tall, broad-shouldered man with a kind face. When Mackenzie nodded to them, they reached into his wagon and lifted out the crates. Then they walked through the crowd, letting everyone take as many of the pamphlets within as they wanted.

As they walked past him, John took a leaflet and scanned the page. "Get your rifles ready," it said at the bottom, "and make short work of it."

Rebellion! So the rumours were true!

The ragged newcomers brushed past John on both sides, beating back a few farmers on their way. A crate of pamphlets fell to the ground, its papers scattered and blown by the wind. Then, before John could see what was happening, the ragged men grabbed the tongue of the wagon and pushed it and its occupant straight towards the nearby bay.

Mackenzie screamed and beat the heads of the bullies with his fists flying. But they just kept on pushing the wagon towards the choppy, grey water.

"Soupets!" shouted one farmer; and then another: "Soupets!"

John knew now who those ragged men were: thugs who

would do almost anything for a bowl of soup. It was well known that the Tories had hired them to threaten voters in the last election. His oldest brother Tobias had told him all about them when the whole family was home for Thanksgiving.

Without thinking, John bounded after the wagon, followed by about a dozen farmers. William Lyon Mackenzie was trying to rescue their country. But right now, John was going to rescue William Lyon Mackenzie from the icy waters of Lake Ontario!

2

John raced through the crowd towards the lake. He reached the wagon first and flung himself on the back of the nearest soupet. The man was caught off guard and tumbled off the wagon into the mud. As he picked himself up out of the mire, he lunged for John, but missed, falling back again into a pile of apple and potato peelings.

Flushed with victory, John jumped on the broad back of another soupet, who was coming to the rescue of his muddy companion. He was not so lucky this time. The soupet turned, swinging, and landed John a heavy blow on the left eye. He staggered back and the man hit him again, right on the mouth.

Now it was John's turn to fall on his back in the sloppy street, scaring a stray pig out of the way.

He was staggering to his feet just as a pack of hefty farmers bolted past and attacked—not a moment too soon. The soupets had pushed the cart right to the brink of the bay, but they were no match for men who'd been lifting hay and struggling with plough horses all summer.

In a few minutes, the fight was over. The soupets were running for shelter and trying to lose themselves in the market crowd. Mackenzie was adjusting his rumpled wig; the two men who had handed out the pamphlets were at his side, and the large one was helping him step down from the wagon.

John scraped a bit of mud off his overalls and straightened his short-coat. As he started up the slope, he held his hand over his jaw and hoped it wasn't swelling too noticeably.

"Laddie!" Was it the voice of the speaker, Mackenzie? He thought he must have imagined it, so he kept on going.

Then someone touched his shoulder. He turned, and had to look down a little at the short, strange-looking man. "You're a grand fighter and I thank you, my boy. You came to my rescue first."

John's face broke out in a huge, beaming smile. "It was nothing, sir."

"Well, I'm Mackenzie, and these"—he pointed first to the large man with the kind eyes and then to the man with the shaggy beard who was struggling with five more farmers to turn the wagon around and pull it back up the hill towards the market—"are my friends Samuel Lount and Peter Matthews. May I ask your name, lad?"

"John Meyers," he said.

"Seems I've heard that name before."

"I was named after my oldest brother and also after my grandfather, John W. Meyers, one of the first settlers around Belleville. But both of them died before I was born."

"Well, they'd have been proud of you today. You're a brave lad, and I thank you." Then off he went to hook up his horse and wagon.

John scrambled up the hill, his heart bursting with joy. The rebels' leader had called him a great lad! Wait till he told George!

As John sprinted into the marketplace, he almost crashed into a gentleman in a frock coat and top hat who was walking away from their wagon.

"Where in the thunder have you been?" George bellowed, staring at John with icy blue eyes.

"Uh…"

"You're covered in mud!"

"You'll never believe it! I—"

"Do you realize what time it is?"

John had no idea. Perhaps twenty minutes had gone by. But then he looked up at the sky, and noticed the sun was so high it must be noon.

"When I said you could look around, I didn't mean for a whole hour!"

"I—"

"No excuses." But his face softened a little as John stood there quietly, holding his left hand over his jaw. "You are a mess. You look as though you'd been run over by a muddy wagon." George grinned. "I'll bet the other fellow looks a lot worse. Now, jump in the wagon. We've got to go."

John hopped into the passenger seat, relieved to be going home. It had been a great day, but now he wanted to get back to Belleville and tell everyone about the Mackenzie adventure.

"You were right about the rebellion," he told George, brandishing his crumpled pamphlet under his brother's nose. But George was not paying attention. He steered Duke and Bonnie up Church to King. Then, to John's surprise, he turned west.

"Hey, where are you going, George?" he said, stuffing the pamphlet in his pocket. "To get home we have to turn east!"

"I have a little business to do before we leave Toronto." They were past the bustle of the market now and the crowds were thinning out, but George spoke in a very low voice. "Now, John, I want you to do *exactly* as I say."

John nodded, but he was starting to get an uneasy feeling.

George pulled a leather pouch from an inside pocket in his brown woollen short-coat. "I put all our market money in this. Here's a horse-blanket pin. Fasten the pouch inside your shirt.

That way if anyone tries to pick your pockets, there'll be nothing there."

George was entrusting the money to *him?* Now John was even more uneasy. "So what exactly is this little bit of business you have to take care of?" he asked, pinning the money pouch inside his brown homespun shirt.

"Just letters from somebody back home that I have to deliver."

As they turned north onto another city street, John wondered what his brother was really up to—and how long this was going to take. "So where are you going with the letters?"

"Oh, not far from here. Near Osgoode Hall, where the Law Society is. I'll leave you on Lot Street, but you'll be able to see the house I'm heading for. If I don't come out in about twenty minutes, then you drive back east to Yonge Street, then go north past the Bloor Tollgate. Stay on Yonge till you reach Montgomery's Tavern. It's on your left. You can't miss the big sign. I know the tavernkeeper there—Mr. Montgomery. He'll be expecting you. If I'm not there by dark, take a room, and stay the night."

"But, George…"

"If I don't come at daybreak, start home. Go at a safe city pace, but when you reach the open country, drive like mad. The horses will be rested then, and with no load it won't hurt them.

I know they aren't pacers, but they're stronger than city horses. Get home with the money as soon as you can. Father needs it."

"He doesn't need it that bad!" argued John.

"Listen, John. There's not much time. There are highwaymen on that road, who'd strip a fellow returning from market to find his money. So stop for no one. Keep going. A youth alone might be a target."

"But I don't *need* to be alone! I can just wait at the inn until you come!"

"No, John," said George, his blue eyes unswerving. "Just keep a cool head, and you'll be safe."

George could be bossy, but this was getting ridiculous. "Is this something to do with Mackenzie and a rebellion?" John asked. "Because if it is…"

Suddenly, George pulled back on the reins and came to a stop. He jumped down from the wagon and threw the reins to John.

"I should be right back," he said. "Now, remember this. If there's trouble here, don't come after me. I'll not recognize you, and you are not to recognize me. Do as I say."

John watched his brother walk south on York Street until he came to a neat, two-storey brick house with a bald grapevine and a gnarled, leafless pear tree in the backyard. Behind that was a shed big enough to stable a couple of horses.

George marched up to the front door and knocked. The door opened promptly and his brother disappeared inside.

John waited.

Two seagulls circled overhead, and a blue jay screamed from the perch in a walnut tree next door to the brick house.

Before long, George came out.

"Well, I'm glad that's over," John said to himself, and the rush of relief he felt told him how afraid he had been.

Suddenly a carriage came speeding down the street past John and turned south onto York. Then it stopped abruptly. Two men in stylish brown frock coats and light-coloured woollen trousers stepped down and walked over to George. They stood on either side of his brother and talked to him for a few minutes. Then they escorted him across the road. George jumped up into the waiting carriage, followed by the men.

Now what's going on? John wondered. Strangely enough, it looked as if George had been expecting the men. John wondered if his brothers, Tobias and Bleecker, knew what George was up to.

John was just trying to decide what he should do when the carriage George had gotten into suddenly turned around and came speeding up towards him. At the last moment it turned and sped back east towards Yonge Street.

"Giddap," John yelled and flipped his reins on the trusty

Duke and Bonnie. But the heavy farm roans were no match for the carriage's fast-paced steeds. The speeding vehicle was soon lost in a blur of horsemen and carriages at Yonge Street.

John's heart sank and his throat went so dry he nearly choked. He bit his lip and swallowed.

But this was no time to panic. He had no choice but to go up Yonge Street to Montgomery's Tavern and wait for his brother. He pulled on the left rein and turned onto the busy road.

Duke and Bonnie clip-clopped along up the hill over the paving stones. Then the small-stoned area gave way to a trail of earth and—John could hardly believe it—mud! John watched the cross streets inch past as the horses struggled heavily up the hill away from the lake. There was no point in pushing the animals. They were doing the best they could. Instead John stewed over George's mysterious actions. George had pulled a fast one on him this time. What was he supposed to tell Mother and Father? That he'd somehow *lost* George in the middle of downtown Toronto? Sure, George had said he'd probably show up at Montgomery's Tavern. But he hadn't sounded very certain.

As Bonnie and Duke struggled past Maitland Street, a horrible thought entered John's head. What if George had not gone willingly, but had been *forced* into that carriage? What if he never got back from Toronto at all? Everyone would blame John,

of course. And if George had disappeared because of the rebellion, it was even worse. He could be hanged for treason and
John would be the last one on the scene who could have stopped
it all....

"Stop, scofflaw! Pay your toll!" John was startled out of his
reverie to see a man in a long, blue plaid scarf and a pair of
patched trousers running out of a low building on his right.

"This is the Bloor Tollgate, you idiot," said the patchy man.
"You pay your toll or you turn right around and go back down
that blooming road. Hand over your shilling!"

"I'm sorry, sir, I didn't notice," John stammered.

"Then you must be one of the Family Compact," the guard
said. "They're good at not noticing things!"

A pair of even more ragged men leaning against the toll-
house fence let out a couple of guffaws, and one of them eyed
John speculatively as he fumbled for his money pouch.

John found the right coin by feel and handed it over.

"Pass," said the patchy man, spitting on the ground beside
John's wagon.

What a dirty old town, thought John. He certainly was glad
he didn't live in Toronto!

3

It was late afternoon when John saw the old two-storey tavern on a slight rise of land to his left. It looked neat and welcoming with its paned windows running along two storeys and facing out onto the street. Just in time. Duke and Bonnie were tired and thirsty and John was getting cold. A chill northwest wind had risen about a half hour before, and dark clouds hung low in the sky, threatening snow.

It had been much farther than he'd thought and it had been uphill all the way. Just north of Bloor, John had stopped to help a man out of a lake of mud that had formed in a hollow in the road. He'd been wary—the man hadn't looked like a farmer, being pale and shifty-eyed. But John had been taught better than to leave an old man helpless. Fortunately a jovial farmer with a couple of heavy draught horses happened by and together they got the heavily-loaded wagon unstuck. After the skinny old gaffer had taken off without a word of thanks, the kindly farmer warned John, "Be careful. Sometimes people just want to get you off your wagon so they can rob you." This made John even more fearful, and when his own wagon had mired down in the mud—three times!—he'd accepted the necessary help somewhat warily.

John turned off Yonge Street and approached the tavern, the smell of roast meat and fresh-baked bread wafting toward him. A large horse trough stood at the south side, from which he let Bonnie and Duke drink. Then he guided them to a hitching post at the side of the tavern. If he decided to stay the night, he'd find shelter, unharness them, and rub them down, but this would do for now.

A wall of smoke and beer smells hit him as he entered the tavern. The room was dark and the few candle-lanterns in the place did little to brighten it up. Streams of pipe smoke filled the room, which made it even more difficult to see anything. But John could see about twenty men sitting on stools, drinking, or at tables, playing cards. The loud, steady noise of men talking and laughing drowned out even the sound of his own rapid heartbeat. He wished George were with him in this room of strange-looking, idle ruffians—though he'd never tell George that in a million years.

"Well, young man, I'll bet you're George's brother." A jolly-looking, mustachioed man wearing a leather vest stepped out from behind the bar. "I'm Montgomery." There was another man serving customers, too. He was short and had straw-coloured hair.

"I'm…" John hesitated. Maybe he shouldn't give his real name.

"You're who?" asked Montgomery.

"Er…John."

"And where's George?" said Mr. Montgomery. "I was expecting him, too."

"He'll be here, er, later." John gulped, then took a breath. "He ran into a friend. They're celebrating, I guess. They hadn't seen each other in years. George really wanted to spend time with this fellow, so he says to me, 'John, you go on, my boy, and I'll catch up with you at Montgomery's.' So he's coming. I'm sure he'll be here before long."

John stopped. He hated lying, and he wasn't much good at it. Mr. Montgomery and the straw-haired man seemed to be looking at him a little strangely. "Er, maybe he got stuck in the mud," he added, a bit desperately. "You know, I got stuck three times on my way up here."

"*That* I can believe," Mr. Montgomery smiled, stroking his moustache. "There's no help from the government on that one. Too busy lining their own pockets to make sure the common man can get from one place to the next!"

"Yeah," said a stocky blond man, wearing a homespun vest.

"I even heard one guy got mired down right up to his waist!"

"That's a tall tale!" said a burly man with a black beard, who was smiling and smoking a pipe.

"Well, Mackenzie told a worse one!" said Montgomery. "Someone here has probably heard it."

"Oh, yeah," said the blond man, his eyes lighting up. "You mean the one where he says he comes upon a hat sitting in the middle of Yonge Street and goes to pick it up and, what d'ya know, under the hat there's a man's head."

"And he asks the fellow…" the black-bearded man interrupted.

"Shut up, Clancy! I'm telling this story, ain't I?"

"Yeah, but not as funny as how Mackenzie does it. He sure is a rip-snorter."

"So, anyways, he asks the guy… 'Kin I pull yer out?' And the guy says, 'Yeah, but you'd better bring a team of oxen, 'cause there's a horse and wagon under me!'"

"That's a good one, all right," the black-bearded man guffawed, slapping his knee. "And that Mackenzie, he sure got the gift of the gab! So where'd you get that shiner, boy?" the man asked John suddenly.

John, startled, looked at Montgomery. The other barman had gone back to wiping cups while Montgomery stood leaning against the countertop, listening to the story and laughing with the men. Now Montgomery patted John's shoulder.

"You just make yourself right at home and wait for your brother to get here." He looked over at the black-bearded man. "Clancy's all right," he told John, then went back to his work.

John took the empty seat beside Clancy. He was a bit gruff but had a jovial, red, windburned face and sparkling brown eyes. He looked like someone John could maybe trust. Better not be too friendly, though. After all, George had warned him, and so had the farmer on the road. And he was carrying a *lot* of money. Impulsively, John rubbed his hand across his shirt and was reassured by the bump. Then he brought his hand down abruptly, afraid of drawing attention to the hidden cash.

"So, where'd you get that shiner?" Clancy asked again. John supposed that by now he did have a black eye, as well as a swollen lip. The whole side of his face was throbbing.

"Oh, it's nothing," John replied boldly. "You should see the other guy!" But he winced when he tried to smile.

The man who'd told Mackenzie's tale was sitting on the other side of Clancy. "You're some kid," he snorted. "That must hurt like hell!"

"It does," John admitted. It was hurting now to talk, and he was still shaking from the cold.

"Here, waiter," said Clancy. The straw-haired bartender came over. "This kid needs something to drink. What'll you have, kid?

Whisky too strong for you?" John supposed it was. Since he was younger, he'd never been one to drink with his brothers. His mother was dead set against liquor, though Father sometimes asked his friends to step out to the barn for a nip or two. His brother Tobias had given him a few swigs of hard cider every so often when he came home to help Father with the harvest. He had liked it. Maybe one drink would help him get rid of the pain, and then he'd be able to eat a little and feel better.

"Cider will be just fine," he said.

"Forget the apple cider," said the straw-haired man behind the bar. "Try a hot toddy! It'll warm you up and kill the pain—if it doesn't kill you first." He laughed at his own joke, but no one else did.

John's teeth were chattering, but he looked straight at the bartender and nodded. No one would know he'd never had a hot toddy before. He wondered what it would be like.

The bartender mixed the drink in a big earthenware mug and plunked it down on the counter. John pushed his hand into the pocket of his overalls for the few pence he'd put there, but Clancy slapped a coin down beside the drink.

"It's on me, kid," said Clancy. "Hope you get feeling better."

"Thanks," said John. He gazed down into the steam spiralling up through the bubbles on the top of his drink. He took hold of the big handle and raised the mug slowly to his lips.

It was too hot to drink fast. So he sipped it slowly.

Clancy slapped down another coin. "Hey, Linseed! Another whisky!" he said.

"It's Linfoot, you clown," said the bartender, "but I'm at your service!" He poured whisky from a square bottle into Clancy's small glass and clapped it back down on the counter. Clancy threw his head back and took it down almost in one gulp. Then he poured himself some water from a pitcher at his elbow and sipped the water more slowly. John looked sideways at him. The man on Clancy's other side was getting up now and heading for the dining room just beyond the bar. Maybe John should follow him and get some supper.

"Are you from a farm around here?" Clancy asked abruptly.

"Yessir!" said John.

"You on your way back home?"

"Yessir! My brother'll be joining me any minute. He could come walking through that door right this very minute, he could."

"So you said," nodded Clancy. "I was only askin'. What's your name?"

"John."

"Well, John, how'd you like to join me for dinner?"

John couldn't believe what he was hearing. A hot meal! Wow! On the other hand, Clancy might be a crook who was out to kill him to get the cash he was carrying inside his shirt. Then John remembered that Montgomery had said Clancy was "all right."

"Thank you, sir," said John. "I haven't actually eaten since this morning!"

"C'mon, then. Let's go."

John slowly followed the black-bearded man towards the dining room. The smell of roast pork and juicy steaks drifted through the doorway. But Clancy walked past the room and straight to the front door. He held it open for John. "I work at an estate just a few miles from here, and the cook makes the best beef stew around. You got a horse, don't you?"

"Two, and a wagon," said John. "But what about my brother?"

"He won't go on without you. Tell Linberg you're going with Clancy and you'll be back in a few hours!"

"You mean Linfoot?" John asked, and hesitated. George had told him to stay here—and he'd never eaten at a tavern before. On the other hand, the place was smoky and stifling, and the very thought of a home-cooked meal made him wild with hunger.

John had waited long enough—it was George's turn to wait. He followed Clancy out the door.

4

"Who's there?" a woman's voice called out.

"It's me—Clancy." John's new acquaintance was knocking on the back door of the large two-storey frame house in the growing darkness.

John stood a few steps behind Clancy, holding Duke and Bonnie by the halter. Clancy's "few miles" turned out to be north on Yonge Street, up hill and down, for over an hour. They'd gotten as far as Hogg's Hollow when they were hit by a sleet storm. Now John was quite sure he'd been led into a trap. The house was elegant, surrounded by flowerbeds almost covered with snow. So the people that lived here were probably upper-class and Tory. He was probably being brought here for questioning about George.

A bolt rattled back and the door flew open. A rosy-faced middle-aged woman in a large mobcap and stiff, white apron smiled at John. "Well, who did you bring with you this time, Clancy?"

"This is John, Maggie—a hungry young man I met at Montgomery's. Hasn't eaten since this morning."

"Well, don't just stand there in the cold. Get your horses put away and come in and eat some roast pork and baked goodies. Mrs. Gibson just bought a wagonload of stuff at the market."

"We're in luck!" said Clancy, his eyes twinkling. "Let's you and me go and get the horses tended to, young John. Then we'll tuck into one of the finest dinners you ever packed away."

"Whose house is this, sir, if you don't mind my asking?" said John as they led their horses out to the stable.

"Gibson's," said Clancy. "David Gibson. He's a surveyor in these parts. I'm his groundskeeper."

Oh, thought John. He still didn't know whether they were friends or enemies.

With Clancy's help, the work of unharnessing, rubbing down, feeding, and watering the two tired horses was done in record time. The familiar smell of roast pork wafted past John's nostrils as the two men stepped into the kitchen. John's mouth was watering! At last!

"Just one minute, John," said Clancy. "Before we dig into supper, there's someone I want you to meet."

Immediately John's mouth went dry. They weren't even going to let him have supper before they questioned him! Clancy started clomping down a narrow hallway that led out of the kitchen into a wider hall covered with thick carpeting and decorated with oil paintings of stern-looking men and women.

The Gibsons don't look like a very appealing bunch, thought John uneasily.

They walked towards the front of the house and Clancy knocked lightly on a large oak door. "Come in," said a voice. Clancy opened the door, and stepped inside the sitting room just ahead of John. A broad-shouldered man with chiselled features, kind grey-green eyes, and very fair hair rose from a bright blue velvet sofa with mahogany arms and greeted Clancy. John stood just inside the doorway and stared around in amazement.

Just above the sofa was a painting of a young woman in a bright yellow dress sitting on an ornate wooden chair. She had large brown eyes and long, dark brown hair that flowed thickly around her shoulders and down her back, almost to her waist. A red felt hat lay across her knees. She looked strangely familiar.

"John...*ahem*, John. This is Mr. Gibson, my employer."

John came out of his trance and blushed slightly as he looked up into the amused eyes of Mr. Gibson, who was now standing in front of John.

"You like that picture, do you?" said Gibson. "So do I. She's my wife!"

John blushed again.

"But welcome to my home, young man," said Gibson, extending his hand.

"He's George's brother," Clancy added, rather abruptly.

"Another of the Meyers boys!" said Mr. Gibson.

John shot a glance at Clancy, then shook hands with Mr. Gibson and eyed him cautiously. How did Gibson know George? Were they all in it together? Were they Tories or Reformers?

He took a deep breath. "Can someone please explain how everyone in Toronto seems to know George and me?"

Clancy guffawed. "Don't worry, son," he said. "I saw you defending Mackenzie at the market today. So I know whose side you're on."

They were Reformers, then. But John was still suspicious. "I'm not on anybody's side," he said. "I just don't like to see a mob closing in on a defenceless man, that's all. And how come you know George?"

"Oh, we've known each other for years. I met him in Belleville years ago."

"And you, sir, when did you meet George?"

"When I was surveying in that area. We surveyors travel around a lot. But now...when did you last see George? We may be able to help."

John retold the story briefly. He didn't see any harm in that. Clancy and Gibson frowned as he told his tale. When he had finished, Gibson said, "Well, John, it looks as if your brother got nabbed by the Tories. He'll be put under lock and key for a few days, I should think—things are happening and I doubt they'd let a spy go till it's over."

"A spy? My brother's no spy, not for anyone!"

"Oh, we're not saying that," Clancy hastily put in. "But he may have been taken for one. Sounds like the house where he delivered the papers was Mackenzie's. He may simply have been delivering local news for Mackenzie's paper, and got caught up in something bigger than he knew."

John looked at Clancy. Then he looked at Gibson. Did they think he was some sort of fool? It was getting more and more obvious that George was mixed up with some rebellion business.

For their part, Clancy and Gibson looked at each other the way his parents did sometimes—as if they were trying to figure out how to tell him something they didn't want to.

"Well, since you're in the middle of all this now…" Gibson said very carefully. Then he stopped himself. "But first, let's decide how we're going to get George out of trouble."

"Oh, don't worry, sir," said John, as coldly as he could. "I'll go and get him out of jail. Just tell me where it is."

"I'm afraid it's no job for a boy," said Mr. Gibson. "What you should do is have a good, hearty supper and a full night's rest.

Then start out for Belleville first thing in the morning, before things get really hot here in Toronto."

Before John could argue, the sitting-room door opened and in rushed a woman in a torrent of words. "Well, finally, David, the baby's asleep. But young Davy was chasing his sisters again…" Then she hesitated. "Oh, I'm sorry. I didn't know you had company."

Mr. Gibson smiled at his wife.

"Evening, ma'am," said Clancy.

Mrs. Gibson stared at John, and John stared back at Mrs. Gibson. She was an older, still beautiful version of the young girl in the picture; and now, John knew where he'd seen her before.

"Dear, this is John Meyers, George's brother. He's come home with Clancy," Mr. Gibson said.

"Well, my goodness. Would you believe it? He's the boy who sold me all those cakes at the market. We are already enjoying your mother's baking," she said. She smiled warmly at John, who blushed.

"That reminds me…the cook is preparing something for us," said Clancy.

"Very good," said Mr. Gibson. "And please find a place for John to stay the night. There's no point in having him go back to the tavern. You're safe here, son."

But John wasn't quite satisfied. "Sir, I must know. Where's

George being held? And who has him?"

"He's probably at City Hall. That's where the Tories are holding their prisoners. I'll send Clancy down tomorrow at day- light to see if there's been any word of him."

5

In his nightmare, John was driving a horseless wagon through the bush north of Belleville, looking for George. Pretty Nan Burditt from the neighbouring farm was sitting beside him, her thick brown hair tucked neatly under her mob cap. She'd just told John that she'd heard George was waiting for them in the Silver Cave. All they needed to do was get there. *Thunkkkmp.* The wagon hit a rock and started sinking down into a quagmire.

John woke up, sweating—partly because of the nightmare and partly because of the thick buffalo robe he was lying under. He rubbed his eyes, wondering why the room smelled like a stable. Then he remembered—it *was* a stable.

Clancy had offered him the spare bedroom in his cottage at the edge of the Gibsons' property, but John had felt the need to be alone—and the need to make a quick getaway in the morning. He and George may have had their quarrels, but he wasn't going to leave Toronto until he'd searched high and low for him.

So he'd slept right in his wagon inside the stable. The hay he'd loaded into the back for a mattress was scratching him this very minute, but he didn't really want to get up. It was chilly outside the buffalo robe—there must have been a frost during the night.

John thought about the dream he'd just had. George wasn't in any Silver Cave—he was just south of here, imprisoned somewhere in Toronto's City Hall. By hook or by crook, John was going to get him out.

And maybe more. Last night, as John had packed away two heaping platefuls of pork, baked potatoes, and creamed vegetables, to say nothing of a couple of pieces of his own mother's apple pie, he'd kept one ear trained on the murmured conversation of Clancy and Mr. Gibson. He had heard Gibson say, "FitzGibbon…urging the governor to act…Rolph…moved up to the fourth…" and then Clancy had burst out, "But it's too soon!" After Gibson hushed him, he went on more quietly, but John had caught the word "provisions."

John figured the rebels were going to attack any time now, and they needed food. Maybe after he'd found George, he'd use his wagon to haul in provisions. He'd be a war courier—like Grandpa Meyers!

John reached down to his feet and found the heavy wool coat he'd brought in case it turned cold. It had warmed up nicely under the buffalo robe. It was convenient, sleeping in a stable. Because he'd slept in his clothes, all he had to do now was get his coat on.

As John fed and watered Bonnie and Duke and hitched them to the wagon, sunlight was just beginning to break in through the cracks in the stable walls. All was still silent at the Gibsons' as John opened the gate and clattered out of the driveway. John turned right onto Yonge Street and headed towards Hogg's Hollow to the south. The muddy old road was now hard and covered with hoarfrost. There'd be no getting stuck three times in four miles on *this* journey. John felt almost happy as his horses clip-clopped over the hardened surface, back to the city.

In the fresh, crisp air, he started to feel hungry. He glanced down at the pack of food that Maggie had insisted on giving him the night before. He pulled it open and was pleased to see it contained some of his mother's baking. He took out a big piece of Christmas cake. More snow was falling now and he thought of Christmas. It wouldn't be long now. Then he remembered it was Sunday morning. The family would be going to church in Belleville, and Mother would be praying for him and George. That made him glad; but it meant that City Hall would be closed. There was nothing John could do for George today.

John saw the white-and-grey tavern looming up before him. He might as well go on in and see if George was there; and if he wasn't, why, John would just enjoy himself a little. He tethered his animals at the hitching post and headed for the front door, but it was locked. Still, there were horses tied to the hitching posts, and so John trudged around to the back door and, sure enough, it was open. A few men were walking in just ahead of him, and when he walked through the door, he could see about twenty gathered and chatting together in the dining room. He went up to the bar and ordered breakfast. Then he sauntered into the dining room to listen to the men talking.

"Did you say that Dr. Rolph is actually thinking of calling off the attack?" said one young man. He was wearing farmer's overalls.

"No. I did not say that," said the man sitting across from the first speaker. He looked like a tradesman from one of the stores that John had passed yesterday on lower Yonge Street.

"Who is Dr. Rolph?" John asked the man beside him.

"Oh, he's a prominent Reformer," came the answer, in an excited whisper. "He's the one Mac wants to head up the new government after the rebels take over. He's really got the bit between his teeth, too—there's talk he's moved up the date of our first skirmish!"

"Yes, I heard he changed it to the fourth," added John, suddenly understanding what he'd heard the night before. "When's that?"

"Tomorrow!" said the tradesman. "Why else would the men be starting to come now?"

A steadier, deeper voice said, "And the men'll be coming all day and all night."

"But we've no arms!" The young farmer's voice rose, and while some looked at him sternly, others cast suspicious glances in John's direction.

Plunk! A huge plateful of fried eggs, potatoes, and bacon landed on the table in front of John. He jumped, then mumbled his thanks. The room was silent while Linfoot went back to the bar.

"Who's the new barman?" someone asked.

John spoke up. "He's called Linfoot."

"Anybody know what happened to Montgomery? He promised to feed the troops."

"Who cares about Linfoot and Montgomery? I want to know what anyone knows about Dr. Rolph's plans." The volume in the dining room rose.

"Never fear," said the older man again. "Rolph sent a man up to tell Lount. He's a blacksmith. I'll bet he has plenty stored at his place."

The young farm boy shook his head. "We don't know that. Lount's a Quaker, you know. He's not for violence."

Lount had been the name of the big man at the market.

John remembered him well.

"Yeah!" shot back another older farmer. "He's no man to lead a rebellion. We sure aren't going to move Governor *Bone Head* without violence of some sort."

"I'm ready to set a stick of dynamite right under him myself," agreed the tradesman.

"Well, Mackenzie will give us some action, all right," said another man, who was picking his teeth.

"Yeah! They're an unlikely pair, Lount and Mackenzie— though they do say that politics makes strange bedfellows."

A round of guffaws followed. A man who had just walked through the door and joined them was looking thoughtful, however. "Strange is the word," he agreed. "Especially when it comes to Mackenzie."

Mackenzie, strange? John thought of the friendly, well-spoken man he'd met yesterday. "How's that?" he almost shouted. A heavy silence fell as the men stared at John.

"I…uhh…heard him speak at the market, yesterday. I thought he was great," John blurted out. The faces of the men relaxed. They smiled at the boy.

"Well, it's like this," the newcomer said. "The man hasn't had much experience with political action. He's a great newspaperman—a journalist. But sometimes he's more 'sound and fury' than anything else."

"Yeah, he yells and shouts a lot at folks, but his heart is in the right place," someone else interrupted. "He wants all men in Upper Canada to be treated the same. If that makes him strange, it's to the Family Compact, not to us!"

The older, well-dressed gentleman nodded in agreement and added, "Mackenzie and Lount aren't in this alone, anyway. They have Rolph and Matthews and others."

"They'll pull together when the time comes. Like all of us. We have a common goal: down with Galloping Bone Head and his Family Compact!"

The men raised their coffee and beer mugs together and cheered.

John cheered with the others, but quietly—there might be Tory spies lurking about, he thought, though no one else seemed to be too anxious about it. He guessed this was a private meeting; but then it was strange that he'd gotten into it so easily.

He stepped over to the bar to pay for his meal. In a minute, Linfoot came out of the kitchen and stared at John across the bar. John plunged his right hand into his pocket and pulled out some change. He hoped the breakfast didn't cost too much.

Linfoot smiled at him and said, "Lad, how would you like to earn your breakfast?"

John hesitated.

Linfoot grumbled, "That Montgomery rented me his tavern and then took himself off before showing me properly how to run the place. I haven't seen him since last night, and I'm short of supplies." John felt sorry for him.

"All right, if it won't take too long," John said.

Linfoot sent him to a farmhouse north of the tavern. The farmhouse was not hard to find, and after he'd unloaded the barrels, Linfoot gave him oats for his horses as well as another meal. John took his time—he'd nothing else to do—so it was well after noon when John got back on the wagon and clucked the horses on to Gibson's. John hoped it was all right if he spent the night there again.

He led his horses past a white pony tied to a hitching post and into the shed. There was still lots of room inside. He unhitched Bonnie and Duke, brought them to the well behind the stable, then returned them to the stable and tied on their feed bags. Then he headed for the house, stomping his feet against the frozen ground.

He knocked loudly and repeatedly. There was no answer. He tried the door and found it unlocked. John walked inside and strode quickly through the now silent and spotless kitchen and into the hall.

He could hear voices through the closed door of the sitting room.

"But why?" a voice was thundering. "I've been recruiting for the *seventh*."

"There's a warrant out for your arrest, that's why! Fitzgibbon was at Government House yesterday, and Bond Head finally realizes you're not all talk. They'll be bringing the troops back from Lower Canada as fast as they can send word there, you can bet on it. Rolph says if we don't march in the morning, we don't march at all!"

"No march! Of course, we'll march!" the other voice exploded.

"We'll get word out to the men somehow, Mac," the calm voice said. "And remember, you promised no violence. Weapons are only for self-defence."

"Ach, of course, of course!" the other—Mackenzie— responded impatiently.

"We can do it, Mac. According to Rolph, the Tories aren't prepared at all. He thinks three hundred of our men could take City Hall, where they've stored the ammunition. Once we have that, the city's ours!"

"But what about food? I arranged with Montgomery to feed the men Wednesday night and Thursday. He'll be prepared for *then*, not now."

Montgomery! Without thinking further, John knocked loudly, and the door burst open.

6

"Montgomery's not there anymore!" John blurted out.

"Who are you?" Mackenzie barked. He seemed to have completely forgotten John.

"Well, young man," sighed Mr. Gibson, "what do you have to say for yourself, eavesdropping like that?" He seemed more resigned than angry.

John realized that listening in at doors was no way to repay a kind host. But he would make the best of it and explain.

"I'm very sorry, sir. I knocked at the kitchen door, but no one answered, so I came on in."

"Who is this boy?" demanded Mackenzie.

"I'm John Meyers from Belleville," John spoke out. "I defended you at the market yesterday."

Mackenzie turned then and gave John his scrutinizing stare. It took a full minute before recognition lit up his face. "Ah, yes, now I remember you, lad. With your black eye and swollen lip, you look…well…different. But I'm the one who's to blame for that," he said. A smile broke across his face as he looked straight at John with his piercing blue eyes. "You're on our side, all right, aren't you?"

John guessed he was, at least for now, so he nodded. "I'm sorry to interrupt you, but I just came back from Montgomery's Tavern. I was looking for my brother. But Montgomery wasn't there anymore." John decided to leave out the part about his running errands. "One of the bartenders is in charge now—Linfoot."

"John Linfoot! He's a Tory!" Mackenzie exploded. "Did you hear any more news, lad?"

"Mr. Linfoot hasn't seen Montgomery since last night."

Mackenzie stared at Gibson in alarm. "What's Montgomery up to?"

Gibson laid a hand on John's shoulder. "Did Montgomery sell out to Linfoot, or just leave him in charge? Think, lad—it's important."

"Oh, Linfoot's just renting, sir," John said hastily. "I remember him saying that."

"Well, then," Gibson assured Mackenzie, "I'll warrant Linfoot will have to honour Montgomery's orders—if he wants." Gibson smiled warmly at John.

"Sir," John spoke up, "I want to find my brother."

Gibson turned to Mackenzie. "John's brother is George Meyers."

"I should have known. Though not too many Meyerses are with us—they're staunch Loyalists, and Church of England." The red-haired man turned to John. "I think George is in jail. He delivered a few pages to my house yesterday. He was followed there and picked up shortly after. But they've got nothing on him. My wife hid the letters he brought and I have them safe— right here." Mackenzie patted the carpetbag beside him on the floor.

"Give them to me!" John rushed forward.

"Don't be crazy, son," said Gibson, reaching for the bag. "This isn't your battle. Stay for the night, then go home. You can't do anything for George. I said before, and I'll say it again— your brother can come to no harm in jail. It's the safest place to be right now. Help yourself to some food from the kitchen cupboards. Then, at sun-up, head for home!"

John grimaced a little, but both men obviously had their minds made up; so he turned and marched from the room.

He hated being treated like a child. Why, he was taller than Mackenzie! John glared at the white pony in the dark on his way to the drive shed. John wasn't sure he admired Mackenzie anymore. What kind of leader would ride a white pony?

John slept in the shed that night, fitfully. He woke once to the sound of Mackenzie untying his pony and riding out into the darkness of the cold December night. Waking again a few hours later, he heard men talking in low tones. In the shadows of the shed, he peered out from under his buffalo robe. About a dozen men were walking silently into the small barn next to the shed. Clancy was among them, so he knew they must be Reformers.

Like himself. As he thought of it, John felt pretty good about being on the Reformers' side. Mackenzie might be a bit crazy, but at least he was defending the underdogs against the power-hogging rulers. Maybe John wouldn't go back to Belleville tomorrow. Maybe he'd march on City Hall with the others. Then he'd liberate George and be welcomed home a hero after it was all over. When he got back to Belleville he was going to tell Nan Burditt the whole story—how he'd saved Mackenzie from drowning, how he'd…John finally drifted off to sleep.

The moon came out from behind a snow cloud and shone down on the wakeful, frightened city below.

***

John woke at about seven in the morning, to the sound of men tramping past the shed towards the house. He opened one eye and looked out from under the buffalo robe. The men didn't look at all like soldiers. They looked just like farmers walking to the house from the barn. None of them even had a musket.

John dressed and leapt down from the wagon. "Morning, Bonnie." John stroked the mare's neck as he led the horses from the stable. "Morning, Duke. Looks like we're heading back to Belleville." He figured Gibson was right. George would be better off without his little brother trying to come to his rescue. Still, he thought it wouldn't hurt to go back to Montgomery's and ask for George just one more time. He had to go south, anyway, to get to the Kingston road—the only route back to Belleville that he knew.

The light snowfall had been followed by a heavier frost, and Yonge Street was firmer now. He was able to trot the horses, and he arrived at the tavern in an hour. Bonnie and Duke were lively and the sun glinted on their red-brown coats. It was Monday, December fourth—only twenty-one days till Christmas. But who knew whether there would even be a Christmas this year?

For the third time in three days, John opened the tavern door. It was starting to be a familiar routine. Except this time, behind the wall of smoke, John noticed a new customer—Mackenzie!

"I pay my debts, man," Mackenzie was shouting. "And I already arranged for the men to be fed here."

The straw-haired Linfoot stooped over and reached under the bar. "I can't find any orders here, sir. You must be mistaken."

Mackenzie leaned over the counter, grabbed the man by his

shirt, and twisted it. "Well, I'm ordering now. The rest of the men will be here around noon and they'll be coming all afternoon. I suggest you be ready—or else," he growled.

The new tavernkeeper was obviously in considerable discomfort. "Where can I find that much food?"

"Find it!" Mackenzie turned away then and almost bumped into John, who was watching right behind him.

"Good morning," Mackenzie said in a civil but disturbed tone of voice.

"Good morning, sir," said John. Then he stepped up to the bar and stared at Mr. Linfoot. "Did my brother George Meyers stay here last night?" he asked.

The tavernkeeper didn't even look at him. "No one stayed the night last night." He went into the kitchen.

"Did you say you did some hauling for this character yesterday?" Mackenize asked him, as John turned away. "That's right! You've got two strong horses and a big wagon. I saw them in Gibson's shed." He tipped his head sideways as though thinking. John stared at the red wig and wondered if it would fall off.

"Lad, I've got a job for you. But it might be dangerous. I really shouldna bother you."

"What can I do?" John asked, his curiosity getting the better of him. They'd have to wait at home a little longer.

"Well, I'm wondering if we may use your team and wagon."

"I guess so, but I have to drive them." Father would never forgive him if he let Bonnie and Duke out of his sight.

Mackenzie jumped up and grabbed the back of John's coat collar. "Let's go!" John almost tipped backwards in his chair, but balanced himself in time and stood on his feet, only to be rushed out the front door of the tavern.

"I'd like to pick up a load at Shepard's Mills. Then we'll go on up to Gibson's." John unhitched the horses and jumped up into the driver's seat. Mackenzie leapt up onto the back of the wagon and stretched out on his stomach in the hay, half hidden in the buffalo robes but looking out over the side.

A short distance before the Gibsons', Mackenzie motioned John to take the road to the left, and they soon came to the mill on the west branch of the Don River. "Stop here," Mackenzie shouted, jumping over the side of the wagon.

John did not have long to wait before Mackenzie was back again, and with him were several men. They had a few dozen muskets and a couple of barrels of musket balls—not nearly enough for three hundred men, John thought, but he said nothing. The men laid the barrels sideways next to the muskets and covered them with the buffalo robes.

"Now to Gibson's," said a grim-faced Mackenzie. The firebrand speaker was subdued and tense. Ten minutes later, they reached the Gibsons' now-latched gate. John tossed the reins to

Mackenzie and jumped down to open it, and Mackenzie drove right on through to the house. John had to run to hop on to the back of his own wagon. Who did this Mackenzie think he was, anyway? Driving recklessly with all that ammunition on board. He was glad he'd come along to protect poor Bonnie and Duke.

"Turn the horses around," said Mackenzie, handing the lines to John. "We're going right back to the tavern." He jumped down, ran up the front steps, and knocked. In only a few seconds, the door flew open and he disappeared inside.

John waited obediently, and about five minutes later, Mackenzie came back out and climbed up beside him. "Gibson and I have errands to run. But I'd like you to take these men and the munitions down to Montgomery's."

About a dozen men came running from the barn and began climbing into the wagon. Some were carrying heavy wooden cudgels. A few held pitchforks.

"Put your weapons down in the bottom of the wagon," Mackenzie commanded. "We mustn't appear to be armed."

Armed? thought John. All they've got is barnyard tools.

Gibson drew up beside John on his magnificent dark brown stallion. "You sure are a bear for punishment, John," said the man, shaking his head. "Don't you realize there's a battle coming up? It could be today, tomorrow, Wednesday, or Thursday—I don't really know. But I do know it's coming, and I don't want you in the middle of it. As soon as you've dropped your load, I want you to head straight for home."

"I will," John said. This time he meant it. He'd done enough for Mackenzie and the Reformers.

But Mackenzie and his doings seemed to cast some sort of spell over John—he didn't know why. Three hours later, he was still at Montgomery's Tavern—wagon, horses and all. What on earth have I got myself into? he thought. Only a week ago, he'd been looking forward to his first trip to Toronto, and now here he was sitting on a load of rebel ammunition.

He was getting more annoyed by the moment, too. Had he been forgotten altogether? The men he'd brought to the inn had all disappeared inside without a backward glance. He'd seen Lount and about fifty other men, tired and tousled, filing into the tavern since then; not one of them had asked why he was sitting there, and he hadn't dared call attention to himself or his load. He didn't even dare fetch water for himself or his horses. Mackenzie had told him not to leave the wagon.

He was getting cold in the frosty air, but he couldn't very well take up even one of the buffalo robes that was hiding his load. Finally, he saw a speck of brown on the northern horizon. It was David Gibson—without Mackenzie.

"Haven't you gone home yet?" Gibson exclaimed as his horse trotted up to John's wagon.

"With this load? How could I?"

"You mean, no one's unpacked the stuff?" Gibson huffed with exasperation. "Drive the horses around back as close as you can to the door. Wait for me there. I'll get help."

Gibson ran inside the front door of the tavern. No sooner had John backed up his horses and straightened up his vehicle than the back door opened wide and he was surrounded by ragged rebels. Gibson threw back the buffalo robes and the men grabbed for the muskets. Gibson and Clancy set one barrel upright and carried it inside. Another two men took the other one.

"You may go now, John," said Gibson. "Godspeed." John nodded. Finally, he was free. He turned onto the road and started south on Yonge Street.

He'd waste no time. He started the horses into a brisk trot.

He hadn't gone far when he heard a sharp ringing command. "Stop!"

Now what? thought John.

"No one passes this point, lad. You'll have to turn back."

John looked into the face of the man beside him. He was dressed in ordinary farmer's clothes but wore a white armband, which identified him as a Reformer. And he was armed, with a musket.

"I'm just going south to take the Kingston road to Belleville, sir. That's home and it's the only route I know to get there."

"Sorry, lad. We have our orders."

Feet apart and gun across his chest, the man stared sternly up at John, who decided it wouldn't be wise to disobey. Sighing, he turned his horses around and headed back up the hill towards the all-too-familiar inn. Perhaps Gibson knew another route to Belleville.

A great rumbling was coming from the front rooms as he walked inside. There must have been more than a hundred men jammed into the space.

"Where have you been?" said a voice behind him. Someone grabbed him on the back of the neck. "I've got a job for you, lad," Mackenzie said in a congenial but firm voice.

Wonderful! John thought. What on earth would this man suggest now?

"An army marches on its stomach. That's what Napoleon said, and he was right!" Mackenzie adjusted his wig, which had tilted over one eye. "In short, we need food, and you're just the one to fetch it—you and that team of yours!"

"Where on earth would I get food?" John shot back. He knew he should show more respect, but things were getting out of hand.

"Just scout around the farmhouses hereabouts. Tell the wives Mackenzie sent you! Tell them about these poor, hungry men,

ready to go into battle for them with no food in their bellies."
Mackenzie put an arm around John's shoulders and lowered his
voice. "That fool Linwood claims he can't leave the place, so
you're our best hope, lad."

He was pleading now. Somehow, John couldn't resist the
man.

"I'll do my best, sir," he said.

He went back out with a heavy heart. He tried to tell himself
this errand wasn't as bad as picking up ammunition. At least the
Tory government couldn't put him in jail for having a wagonful
of victuals! Or could they? Was feeding the rebels an illegal act?

***

It was dusk when John arrived back at the tavern, but he was
pleased with his haul: potatoes enough to feed 150, vegetables,
and cooked and uncooked meat. He even had a couple of crates
full of live hens. He had been surprised at how willing people
around were to contribute—he hardly had to ask. A lot of farmers apparently supported the rebels, even if they weren't willing
to march themselves. They were eager for news, too, which was
why it had taken so long.

John parked by the back door and slipped inside. The front
rooms were crammed with noisy men. As he was craning his
neck to look into the crowd, he almost stumbled into Mr
Linfoot. "Mackenzie sent me for food," he said. "It's out back."

"I'll get men to help," Linfoot said. John had to wonder about the new proprietor. Was he a spy? Was Montgomery? Not for him to figure out, he thought, as he went out again to tend to the horses.

By the time he came back from the well, men were gathered around his wagon like a swarm of grasshoppers. He hated to see all those pies, cookies, dried apples, chicken, beef, and winter squash disappear into the kitchen. His stomach growled, as if it agreed with him.

"You've done a good job, boy," said Linfoot. "Sit down now and eat your fill."

"I'll do that. I haven't eaten since morning."

The tavernkeeper looked at him with surprise. "You mean you didn't help yourself to some of this?"

"No, sir. It wasn't given to me."

"Well, for that you must take extra with you for the road. I insist. Have a piece of this pie while I pack it up for you."

A number of men were washing potatoes and throwing them into pans unpeeled. Others were axing off chickens' necks and cleaning out their insides. The smell was quite overwhelming. The men talked as they worked.

"How long do you figure it'll take the troops to get back here?" asked a young fellow in the far corner. He wasn't any bigger than John, though he was probably nineteen or twenty.

"Well, they'll stay to lord it over Papineau awhile, no doubt."

So the rebels in Lower Canada had been defeated! John wondered what Father and Tobias and Bleecker would say about that—or George, if he'd heard the news. John's chewing slowed as he listened more intently.

"Yeah, but you can bet on it that the government will send someone post-haste to tell them to hightail it back here. I'd say we have a few weeks—but that's time enough." That fellow sounded more hopeful. But John knew they were all feeling worse now. The entire success of the uprising depended on them, and it was really too early to strike. The Reformers need-ed at least a few more days to get ready.

Cra-a-a-ck! Crack! Crack! Gunshots! They were close—too close, thought John. It sounded like they were right in front of the tavern.

The room fell silent. The men looked up from their work and stared at each other. Some of them looked scared. Others just stood paralyzed. The pie John had just eaten did a flip in his stomach.

"I'll see what's going on," said Linfoot. He swung the door back and went into the front bar. Too bad he's a Tory, thought John. He's a decent fellow—and brave, too.

In a few minutes, the tavernkeeper came back. "It's all right.

Just a couple of fellows trying to break that picket line you set up outside."

The men returned to their work and the talking started up again—but not as loudly as before. John poked a potato in one of the pots. It was still hard. He helped himself to a chunk of cold roast pork, some bread and carrots, and an apple. He didn't want to eat there in all that smell and noise, so he took his plate and sat down on a low barrel in a storeroom off the kitchen.

At last, peace and quiet. John was just lathering a chunk of butter over his bread when the door burst open. Two men were carrying in a groaning man. They laid him on the floor at John's feet. He was dressed in a full military uniform, and John gasped. Blood was dripping steadily from a tear on the left side of the man's jacket. He'd been shot.

"Out of here, boy," said one of the men. John fled back into the kitchen. Was the whole tavern going to become a slaughter-house? He set down his plate on the nearest table and headed for the door. But someone reached out and grabbed his arm. "Not so fast, boy. You're going to stay and help Linfoot. Tomorrow all the men will be fighting, and they'll need grub more than ever."

Linfoot walked over to John. "You'll be inside, son. You won't be in the line of fire at all." Linfoot looked tired and worn.

"But what about my horses?"

"We'll keep them inside our sheds. They'll be safe and warm.

73

I'll see to that. It's only for a few days, John. This little crisis isn't going to last. Too bad it had to happen at all."

John sighed as he slashed away at the potato he was peeling. He didn't want to be here, at all. He was a prisoner, really, and these men had no right to keep him. One thing was certain, he wasn't hungry anymore after what he'd just seen. He just wanted to be out of all this and on his way home. He was more worried about himself now than George. His brother would have to take care of himself. After all, it was George's fault he was in the middle of this battle.

Where would they all sleep tonight? The tavern wasn't big enough. He'd have to get to his wagon before anyone made it their sleeping place. And then, when the place was quiet, he'd head straight for home.

7

It was almost eleven o'clock on Tuesday, December fifth, and John was wedging his way through the tightly packed crowd of men in the yard and road in front of Montgomery's Tavern. It looked as if there were hundreds of men milling about in front of the tavern, all wearing white armbands.

He'd worked late into the night before he collapsed on a cot in the kitchen. When he woke up this morning, he'd changed his mind again. He would check on George before he left for home. Then, all morning, John had been washing dishes and peeling potatoes, and now he figured his part in the rebellion was done. With his team and wagon safely stowed in the tavern shed, John was going to look for City Hall and George. This time he was going on foot, so he could get around the pickets. With all the coming and going, no one would notice him.

He broke through a line of men and found himself facing Mackenzie astride his white pony, prancing about a little to keep the throng from crushing in against him. He wore several over-coats, and the outer ones were far too big for him. In fact, the biggest outer one was pulled right up to the tops of his ears and up over the bottom of his chin. But his mouth was uncovered and he was using it.

"Brave Canadians," Mackenzie shouted. There was a cry of approval from the men. He continued. "There are rich men now as there were in Christ's time. A wicked government has tram-pled the law, has declared that they will roll their fine carriages and riot in their palaces at our expense; that we are poor, spirit-less, ignorant peasants who were born to toil for our betters. But the peasants are beginning to open their eyes and feel their strength...."

While every eye was focused on Mackenzie, John made for the road. He started into a run; and, just as suddenly, he came to a swift halt. A running man might be stopped by a bullet.

After a while, John jumped the fence and crept along under cover of some cedar bushes. He had to do his best to avoid the pickets altogether rather than get through one. The wounded man they dragged into the tavern last night had been trying to pass through a picket. And he'd died. Colonel Moodie was his name—the first victim of the rebellion.

As he neared the picket line, he saw that not only the road, but the whole area around the picket was well guarded. He sat down to think for a bit. Then he wrapped a white handkerchief around his left arm and tied a scarf over his face. He stuffed almost all his red hair under the cap he'd crammed into his coat pocket. He'd join a group of rebels when they marched down Yonge Street, then cut loose as soon as he could.

The sun was high overhead. It was noon. John glanced back and saw figures in the distance. The men were starting to come down the street. They did not march like military men; some stepped out briskly in long strides, but most plodded along in their heavy, high boots and held their weapons over their shoulders—pitchforks, shovels, long-handled axes, and homemade spiked clubs. Their bulging homespun coats were secured with flapping woollen scarves, and their baggy patched trousers hung loosely. Samuel Lount and his men were the vanguard. Mackenzie and his white pony were close behind.

John broke a heavy branch from a tree and whittled the end sharp with his pocket knife. Then he hopped back over the fence, flung his weapon over his shoulder, and fell in with Lount's men. He was as tall as some of them and he was certain he looked at least eighteen. The men walked freely past the picket line with John on the outer fringe.

He followed along with the others for about half an hour, walking briskly while looking for a way to jump the fence and get out of the crowd. Just before Gallows Hill, Lount signalled his men to stop. While Lount addressed his men, John started inching back and searching for a place to slide into the bushes.

"Remember," Lount was saying, "we are Mackenzie's vanguard, but we are not men of war. We carry arms only for self-defence. We will attack no one. Remember, men—only for self-defence. We are marching on City Hall only to voice our dissatisfaction with the government's favouritism and unfair taxation."

John slipped down behind a small embankment and Lount's men strode on. He didn't move a muscle until Mackenzie's white pony paced by—with more men clad in homespun, carrying arms as feeble as those of the vanguard. John reflected on Lount's words. Somehow, he didn't think Mackenzie was of the same opinion as Lount. What on earth was going to happen to these two leaders? Would they clash in the middle of a battle?

When everyone had passed, John knocked off the sharp part of his staff. On Toronto's terrible roads, walking sticks were common. He took the white handkerchief off his arm, but kept the scarf over his freckled nose and the cap on his head. Even at a distance from the road, his flaming hair might give him away.

At Gallows Hill, hundreds of men were standing tall, their white armbands reflecting the colour of Mackenzie's pony. Surely, John thought, the officials in town would recognize this was a peaceful march of protest: white had always been a symbol of peace and parleying. He heard the crowd erupt into murmurs. He looked to the south. There, coming over the brow of the hill, were two white flags.

Good! thought John. He could make some distance now that everyone's attention was elsewhere. He broke into a run.

***

After a couple of hours cross-country, John got tired. Sneaking past farmhouses and struggling over ploughed, frozen fields took too much out of him, he decided. He might as well walk right on Yonge Street, ready to hide if he saw or heard anyone coming.

He hopped the fence again, and glanced up and down Yonge Street. It was strangely empty and, except for the Tory guard that had been posted at the crossroads, so was the concession road to the south of him. There were gardens around the nearby large estates, but they were frozen over. Only a few old vines and straggling winter crops remained. John looked at one large brick home and thought he saw eyes peeking out from behind front-window curtains. Then the silence was broken by the harsh and irregular clanging of church bells. It was an ominous warning to everyone.

Before long, to his surprise, the rebels came into sight, lumbering along down Yonge Street with their white armbands picking up the sun's afternoon rays. Grinning, John tied his handkerchief back on his arm and shouldered his staff again. As the men came closer, he hesitated. They were grim and scowling, not laughing and relaxed as they had been before.

Just before the concession road the band of men turned into a large estate. John followed along on the other side of the thick hedge that lined its drive, then crept around the drive shed. Tied up in front was a white pony.

What was going on? What was this place? Hoping to find out, John went quietly back along the hedge, then paused. Some of the men were talking. John strained to hear their low voices.

"What are we waiting for? Let's chase Dr. Horne out of his comfortable bed and burn the place down, like Mac promised!" growled one voice.

"And give Bone Head a reason to hang us?" asked another.

"He means to anyway! Why else withdraw his offer of amnesty?" said a third.

"That parley meant nothing, either way," said the second voice. John recalled the white flags at Gallows Hill. Had that been an offer of truce from Bond Head? "The law's on our side if we keep the protest peaceful," the second voice went on. "Burning down the house of the governor of the Bank of Upper Canada is a horse of a different colour."

"So you're for Lount, then?" the growler challenged.

"Parleying with the likes of Sheriff Jarvis until you're blue in the face?"

"I'm for rebellion. What Mackenzie wants seems like revenge to me." The voice was mild still, but with a thread of steel.

Before the growler could answer, John heard shouts. He raced alongside the hedge towards the drive shed and peeked around it. He could see the side of the house. Smoke was billowing out of a window toward the back.

John was shocked. Did Mackenzie really mean what he said, then? Somehow, he had thought the newspaperman's fiery words were just that, words, much akin to action as his fiery red wig was to John's own hair.

Time to get out of here, he thought, edging over to the side of the house. He'd go over the fence on the other side of the house next door, across the concession road and away.

Mackenzie came staggering out of the house just then, with his handkerchief over his mouth. He was followed by a band of servants, shivering women, and crying children. Mackenzie raised his arms and motioned his men towards the house next door. John followed back of the houses, intending to beat a path for the concession road immediately. But curiosity got the better of him. He found a place where he could watch, yet stay hidden, just in time to see Lount emerge from the second house.

He stood on the front stoop and spoke in a loud, clear voice.

"I have spoken with Mrs. Jarvis, who has informed me there are sick people in this house. I have assured her that our battle is not with women and children and not with the sick. We will not enter here."

"No!" shrieked Mac, running up the steps. "We will not harm the women or children, but why should we leave our enemy their soft beds to sleep in this night while we have hardly any place to lay our head? Brave Canadians, forward march!" Mackenzie motioned wildly with his arms for his men to follow. "If you will not, I alone shall burn this house as I did the last!" He plunged ahead to the front door.

He banged squarely into Lount, who had not moved. The big man stood passively and rested his hand on Mackenzie's shoulder with a firm grip. Little Mac stared up in shocked astonishment. His red wig fell off, but his face was still red, with rage.

"I will not stop you," Lount began. "I am going to walk down these steps and to my men. If you go inside this house, I will take my men and leave for home. And we will not return! I have given my word to the mistress of this house and I will not be overruled. I will not fight you. I will return home and my men will go with me. Make your choice, Mackenzie."

Lount took his hand from Mac's shoulder and without looking back, he walked briskly down the steps.

A startled Mackenzie stood staring after Lount. Then he

turned and raced after him. "Where's my pony?" he shouted. "Get my pony! We'll march on down Yonge Street."

John stayed no longer, but bolted across the concession road.

***

The streets of Toronto were quiet, and at first, John walked them openly. But then he came upon a strange assembly of men, crossing a side street before him. He shrank into a doorway, and watched them pass: some were young, probably students; some were older, dressed like gentlemen or gentlemen's servants. Some were white; quite a few were black. All were carrying muskets. John tried to guess how many there were. He thought about four hundred, not quite as many as the rebels, but all well armed!

"…I hear these rebels are five thousand strong," one was saying. "They'll chop us to pieces with their axes."

"That's no talk for an Upper Canada College cadet," said an older man. "We'll make a good show with our muskets, training or no training."

"Bond Head should have taken Mackenzie's activities seriously a long time ago," said another man. "Instead he just dismissed anyone who mentioned the word 'rebels.'"

A well-dressed young man, tall with a big nose, laughed aloud. "Like Cleopatra—he whipped the bearer of bad news!"

"Ha! Ha!" guffawed another volunteer. He shook the tall

young man's hand vigorously. "Rose is the name. And you are...?"

"John A. Macdonald. I have a law practice in Kingston..."

Just then one of the stragglers caught sight of John.

"You there, lad! Where are you going?"

"I'm just..." John's voice squeaked with fright.

"How old are you, lad? Old enough to fight for King and country?" asked a kindly, older gentleman.

"I'm fifteen. I'm...I'm on my way to fetch the doctor. My mother's ill..." John hoped the men would believe the lie. Fortunately, they seemed to take his obvious fear as concern for a sick mother.

"Be on your way, then, lad, but don't dawdle. There are rebels about!"

John sped past them, thanking Heaven that he had taken the white handkerchief off his arm. Keeping to side alleys and back gardens from then on, John was a long time in getting to City Hall. It was almost dark when he reached it, and the front door was locked.

John circled to the back of the building to see if a door might open there. As he was going around, he glanced down, and found himself looking directly into a basement window— open, but covered with bars. He peered into the darkness inside, and saw a bent head covered with wavy dark hair.

"George!" he said in a low voice. The head looked up—it *was* George! They locked eyes for a moment, then hands reached up and slammed an inside shutter across the barred window.

Before anyone could come out and seize him, John darted away. He ran at top speed, not stopping until he got back to Yonge Street. At last! Even though he couldn't do anything to help George, this trip to City Hall had not been wasted. He knew George was alive, at least for now. And John was ready now to do as George had told him at the beginning—to go home to Father.

8

"Halt! State your business!"

The darkness deepened into a solid shape, and suddenly John was confronted by a musket-wielding boy hardly older than he was, by the look of him. And the sound—his voice had gone high from excitement.

"What have we here?" asked another, calmer voice. A smoky lantern was lifted to reveal a kindly face that looked familiar. "Why, it's you. You've been a long time. Where's the doctor?"

John swallowed hard. "He…he was with another patient. I waited awhile, but then he sent me home to stay by my mother until he comes."

"Let me take you," said the kindly gentleman. "The streets are dark, and Sheriff Jarvis's men are likely to take anyone they meet wandering for a rebel, even a little fellow like you." He laughed, for he meant to make a joke: John was taller by an inch than he was.

But John was too frightened to laugh. In the light from the lantern, he could see a great mass of men and hear their murmurings and occasional shouts from commanding officers.

"It's all right. My home is just down there." John pointed in a vague way down Maitland Street. "I must go. My mother will be anxious about me...." He darted off. That last part, at least, was not a lie. John was sure that by this time, Mother must be frantic.

At the first alleyway, John cut north again. Tramping sounds seemed to be coming from every direction. What was going on? Would there actually be a battle right here at Maitland and Yonge Street?

If so, John had to get out of the line of fire. In his haste, he tripped over a frozen watermelon but righted himself and scrambled into a stairwell covered by a cellar door at the side of the nearest house. He crouched there, his heart pounding, while the tramping sounds drew nearer. In a few minutes he almost leapt out of his skin with fright. A low voice spoke out of the darkness.

"We're almost there. Do not fire first, but if they fire at us, we will return their fire. But wait for my command. Then fire in unison!"

Men stepped forward and moved slowly to the end of the very garden where John was hiding. But what men? What light there was glinted off metal here and there. Was that a pitchfork tine, or a musket with bayonet? In his fear, John even forgot which was north and which south.

From one side of the darkened yard, John heard someone shout, "Fire!" A torrent of shots, and then—

"Fire!" came the answer from the other side.

The men in the garden turned and ran. One of them was running towards John. Instinctively, John raised the door, and the man jumped in beside him.

"It's Sheriff Jarvis and his picket! They've flattened our whole front flank," he said, shaking. "We're in retreat." John sat very still and said nothing. Finally, he dared to crack open the door and look out. All he could see were men running in all directions. No one was paying any attention to the furious figure on the small white horse.

"Come back, you idiots! Cowards!" It was little Mac! John turned back to his companion in hiding, intending to ask what Mac was planning now. But the man was staring at him, eyes narrowed.

"Wait a minute. Whose side are you on?"

Too late, John remembered his white handkerchief, tucked safely in his pocket.

"I…I…" John's mind whirled. If he identified himself as a rebel, he'd be in trouble for deserting his post at the inn kitchen, or taken for a coward for not fighting. But if he didn't…The image of Colonel Moodie's bleeding body came to mind. Suddenly, anger replaced his fear. Surely he'd done enough for this mixed-up rebellion!

"I'm not on any side! I'm just trying to get home! I've been stuck in this city for days, all because of my brother!"

The man raised his sharp-pointed staff. "Who's your brother?" he barked.

"George Meyers! He's being held prisoner right now by the Tories. Ask Mac!"

The man poked John with his staff. "I reckon I will," he said. "But first, I'm taking you prisoner."

So John was marched back up Yonge Street to Montgomery's Tavern, cold, hungry, and tired. At least it wasn't at staff-point the whole way. The excited rebel soldier jabbed him along for a mile or so, and then they encountered Clancy. The poor rebel slunk away to the sound of the black-bearded man's roaring laughter. Clancy laughed until the tears ran down his cheeks, clapping John on the back until he quite forgot the pain from the sharp-pointed staff.

It was the only bright spot of the whole miserable, long night. A late meal of biscuits and potatoes with watered-down rum did nothing to impress the men. And sleeping space, once again, was limited. Men snored, yelled out in their sleep, and complained of the cold, hard, wooden floors. As if this weren't bad enough, Mackenzie prowled about, stepping over the sleeping men, checking on—well, John didn't know what.

There were a lot fewer men the next morning. Lount persuaded them to remain one more day to wait for the rest of the Reformers to join them, and sure enough, more came. At eight o'clock Thursday morning, Anthony Van Egmond, an experienced military leader, arrived at the tavern with five hundred men. At last, the rebels did not have to rely on the leadership of a lunatic perched on a pony!

When the men marched off to fight again, they left John up to his elbows in dish soap and dirty plates and under the watch of a toothless gaffer whose hands were hard and whose rheumy eyes were surprisingly sharp. By afternoon, the battle had come closer. Even amidst the kitchen clatter the occasional gunshot could be heard. Then David Gibson came in with guns in both hands levelled at a clutch of prisoners.

Thanks goodness! thought John. Reinforcements! To his joy, Gibson had a new job for him. "We've lost," said Gibson, grim but noble. "And they're going to burn my home. Hitch up your horses as fast as you can, John, and gallop straight north to warn my wife. Then take her and the children to her sister's place— she knows the way. She'll be safe there."

"Yes, Mr. Gibson," said John, dropping the pan he was

scouring in his haste to whip off his apron. The sound of gun-shots was coming nearer and nearer all the time. "But where will you go?"

"That I can't tell you, John, but I'll not be staying here!"

John set off up Yonge Street, trotting Bonnie and Duke as hard as he could, turning only once to look back to the southern horizon. A red glow had spread over the whole sky.

Montgomery's Tavern was burning.

9

Never in all his life had John's home looked so beautiful, even bathed in moonlight.

After two long days of pulling the wagon along rutted country roads, Bonnie and Duke turned happily into the Meyerses long farm lane a little past midnight and trotted up the familiar knoll in front of the house, stopping in front of the grove of spruces that stood at the west end of the dooryard. They were ready for a well-deserved bag of oats followed by a good, long sleep. And John felt about the same as his horses— apart from the bag of oats. It seemed like he had been gone for longer than a week. So much had happened, he hardly felt like the same person.

With a volley of happy barks, John's collie, Boots Jr., raced towards him. John hopped from the wagon and braced himself for an enthusiastic greeting. It didn't come. To John's shock, a figure stepped from the shadows and sent the poor dog sprawling on the snow with a practised kick.

It was a military figure in a red coat.

"Who are you?" the soldier demanded.

"What do you mean, 'Who are you?'" said John. He was hungry, furious, and tired. And this was *his* home. "It's more like 'Who are *you?*' And what are you doing here? You're trespassing on private property!'"

Boots came whining back to the edge of the wagon, where John gave him a reassuring scratch behind the ears. This was really too much.

"I'm still waiting," said the soldier in his officious tone.

"You have no business…" John started, then saw two more soldiers step up beside the first one. He looked up towards the house. Father was coming down the knoll from the back, followed by Bleecker and Tobias. What were *they* doing here?

"Is that you, John?" said Father, pushing the tail of his night-shirt down into his trousers as he hurried forward. He was a big, straight-backed man of sixty and he cut an imposing figure.

"This is my youngest son, John," Father announced in a loud, firm voice. "He's been doing business for me, delivering produce. We have regular customers."

"Why weren't we told about him before?"

"You never asked."

"Well, he's sure coming in late in the day."

"Yes, it is late. And we all need to get up early in the morning. Just let us bed these horses down for the night and get back to the house. We'll answer all your questions in the morning." To John, he said, "You go on up to the house, John. I'll take care of the horses. You've had a long day."

"You mean he's had a long…" Tobias began, then clamped his mouth shut as Bleecker mumbled something in his ear.

"C'mon in, John," said Tobias. "We've got something to tell you."

The head soldier tightened his lips and the other two stared long and hard as Father took his time leading the team towards the barn. John followed his two oldest brothers into the house, glad that they were home. Like George, they could be a bit bossy sometimes; but at times like this, bossy people and the way they took charge were a relief.

"What were you going to tell me?" asked John as the three of them stomped up the back steps and into the big farm kitchen, shaking the snow off their jackets.

"We were going to tell you," said Bleecker, "that your mother has been worried sick. Where the Devil did you get to? And where's George?"

Mother—small, with a grey-streaked mass of brown hair tied in a knob at the back of her head—was standing over the big wood stove just to the right inside the back door. She looked up when they came in and and didn't seem to recognize John. He could see her eyes were red—probably from crying over him.

"John! My baby! It's really you!" She ran over to her dirty, scraggly fifteen-year-old son and hugged him tight.

"I'm all right, Mother. Don't fuss!" said John. But he patiently endured the hug. He guessed she needed it.

"Don't fuss? You were supposed to be back here days ago. And with tales about rebellions…and people getting shot and killed…"

"Yes, John, you sure picked a good time to run away from home. Mother's been out of her mind with worry," said Tobias, leaning against the doorway into the dining room.

"Well, it's all right now that you boys are home," said Mother. "Sit down and I'll give you a great big slice of apple pie." She peered over John's shoulder and called, "George, come on in! I won't scold! There's lots of pie for you, too!"

John felt sick. In his relief to be home, he had forgotten about his brother. He sank onto one of the long benches at the side of the wooden table. "Mother, u-h-h…"

"What, John? What's happened to George? Tell me, boy. Tell me now." Mother set the pie plate down carefully on the bare boards of the table. Her hands were shaking.

"He's safe, Mother, don't worry. He just didn't come home with me yet."

"What do you mean, yet? Where is he?"

"He's...well, he's in jail!"

"He's *what?*" said Father, striding through the back door.

It was the worst possible way for Mother and Father to find out what happened. And with Tobias and Bleecker here, too, thought John. But then again, would there have been a good way to break the news?

Mother burst into tears. "Well, this is the living end," she sobbed. "My own sons—runaways and felons." Despite her tears, she managed to cut John a big piece of pie, pour them all mugs of tea, and settle herself in the rocking chair by the stove. She wiped her eyes with her apron and got out her knitting. "Well, John, you might as well tell us the whole story now," she said.

Father stepped past Mother and sank down on the straw-filled couch, skilfully upholstered with heavy burlap bags that had been dyed a rich green colour. They all stared at John. So he began: "Well, it was like this. We arrived at the market as scheduled, but afterwards..."

When John had finished the whole tale of events in Toronto, a silence hung heavy in the big room. The green muslin curtains rustled only slightly in the drafts from the windows.

Tobias huffed loudly. "I suggest we pray hard while we get a message to Grandpa's old crony, Bishop Strachan, and get our little brother blasted out of jail by one of the most influential Tories in Upper Canada," he said.

"Yes," said Bleecker, who was deep in thought. "If, as John says, George was merely delivering some unspecified papers to Mackenzie, there's very little his accusers can bring forward. If John had just been able to speak with him…"

John stared down at the crumbs on his plate, feeling horrible.

"John," said Mother, looking at him as if he were eight years old, "we're glad you're back. And you tried your very hardest. Really, you were kidnapped, too."

He knew Mother was trying hard to make him feel better, but everything she said only made him feel worse. If he hadn't loitered with the rebels on Monday, he would have been able to visit George when City Hall was open. George could have given him a message to pass to his family, perhaps vital information to use in his defence.

"Well, there's little we can do until the soldiers leave," Father pointed out.

"Father, what are those soldiers doing in our sheds?" John asked.

"They're the military men coming back from Lower Canada."

"Why didn't they go by steamer? It's faster, and everyone said Head was waiting for them in Toronto."

Father looked at John sharply, then nodded. "Not these ones. They were sent overland specifcally to spy around."

"Do you think there are any real rebels from this district?"

Once again, Tobias and Bleecker exchanged a quick glance but said nothing.

"There are lots of bigmouths and complainers," said Father, "but I doubt if any from the Midland District were involved in the Toronto battle."

"Except John," came a little voice from the back stairs, and everyone turned to look. Sarah Ann swung open the door. Still half asleep, she was rubbing her left eye and squinting at every-one in the flickering light of the coal-oil lamp. That, and her long blonde braids which hung past her waist, made her look younger than her thirteen years.

"Sarah Ann!" cried Mother. "Get back to bed! You'll catch your death!"

"The soldiers like Mother's cooking," said the girl calmly, and she strode into the room as if she sat up late listening at doors every night. "Especially her fruitcake! Welcome home, John," she added with a smile. She poured herself a mug of tea and sat down beside Father. Mother threw up her hands.

John smiled right back. He had to admit it was nice to see

his pesky little sister again. He turned back to Father.

"How many are there?"

"About a dozen—and your mother gave them a meal fit for the King," said Father. "Without you and George, and with only Jane and Sarah Ann at home, she complains it's too quiet."

"How long have the soldiers been here?"

"They only arrived late this afternoon. So far they've stayed out in our sheds—except, of course, at supper. They were very respectful," Father added thoughtfully. "They kept telling your mother what a good cook she was until she kept offering them more and more fruitcake."

"*My* fruitcake!" said another voice. It was Jane, wrapped in a shawl and coming downstairs to see what all the commotion was about. "John Meyers! Where've you been?"

"John's been trapped in the middle of a Toronto uprising, Jane," said Bleecker.

"Well, isn't that something!" said Jane, putting her hands on her solid hips and brushing back her thin blonde hair. "Not only do you get lost for a week and drive us all crazy with worry, but what do you do it for? For that hare-brained rebellion. If people would just obey the authorities and sit and talk things out when they need to—"

"Calm down, Jane," said Mother. "John's back in one piece and that's the important thing."

Jane stood right beside John now and tapped his shoulder. She was a tall, solid girl with a strong voice. "And worse, because of all this, my wedding has been delayed to the day before Christmas. And all on account of a bunch of ruffians. I suppose now our dear bishop will be so busy dealing with the hoodlums he won't be able to marry me for another month!"

"You're marrying the bishop?" said Tobias, winking at John.

"Where's George?" asked Jane, ignoring Tobias.

"He's been detained—by the Tories!" said Tobias.

Jane peered at him. "Are you serious? But he's the best man. You mean he isn't going to make it for my wedding?"

"He may not get here at all!" John shot back. "He's in a jail at City Hall!"

"He's deserted me," wailed Jane.

John was disgusted. "Oh, sure," he snapped, "he got himself jailed so he wouldn't have to stand up at your wedding. Think of someone else for once! George is in danger!"

Sarah Ann's eyes grew wide.

"That's enough, " said Father sharply. "George is safe for now. All we need is a little time to see about things."

"I'll keep on helping with chores," said Tobias, "but I have twenty head of my own to milk. Maybe Bleecker could help—if he hasn't forgotten how to milk a cow."

Tobias farmed not far away, but Bleecker was a doctor, with a practice in Belleville.

"You know I'll help, but I get called out at all hours—day and night," he said. "Still, I'll come when I can. Though I don't see any reason why John and Jane can't manage."

"Me!" Jane was outraged. "It's all I can do to plan my wedding! Why, tomorrow, I'll be at Nancy's all afternoon getting my wedding dress fitted, even if it is Sunday. I won't have time to milk."

"Nancy…" said Bleecker thoughtfully. Their sister was married to Caleb Gilbert, a nearby farmer. Perhaps he could help.

"I'm going to bed," said Jane. "We can talk about this in the morning. Come along, Sarah Ann."

Yawning, Sarah Ann got up to follow her sister up the stairs. But Father stopped them. He looked around the room, catching each one's eye in turn.

"Just one thing more," he said soberly. "In case you're asked, John was delivering potatoes to his sister Mary in Belleville yesterday. Bleecker, you see her first thing in the morning to update her on things."

"I will, Father, and now, I'd better get back to Hanna and the children," said Bleecker. He headed for the door.

"Wait for me," said Tobias. "We can harness our horses at the same time. Now, Father, I'll check in with you in the morning after I've finished the chores. At least, you have John home now to help."

"Thanks, son. A safe trip to both of you." He turned to Mother. "You go on upstairs now. The soldiers will want their breakfast early. John and I will clear these dishes away."

Mother sent her husband a grateful glance and hurried upstairs. As soon as she was gone, Father laid a hand on John's arm.

Before his father could say a word, John unfastened the pouch of cash from inside his shirt and handed it over. "It's all there—every last penny," he said.

"And it'll come in handy with the times ahead," said Father, "You managed very well, John. And to think it was your first visit to Toronto! I'm proud of you. Now I have some advice for you. You were not a willing part of this rebellion. You only did what they ordered you to do. So you are no rebel. Still, I advise you not to tell a single person about what happened."

"But, Father—"

"I know you'll be wanting to brag about it to your friends, but you must not."

"Well, I wouldn't say *that*, but I did want to tell—"

"This is serious. No matter what the cause, it's treason if you participated, at least while the present government is in control. We don't know who's on whose side anymore, and mark my words, it's not over yet. Well, let's turn in."

John followed his father up the stairs. At the top, Father turned the wick of the lamp down low and, reaching up, placed it in the hall wall-bracket.

John undressed quickly, chilled by Father's words. The hall lamp gave him just enough light to see by, though he could feel his way around in this room. There was only the big bed that he used to share with a brother, and the little chest of drawers for his clothes, which stood against the far wall.

John lay down, his mind far too active for sleep. Would his brother be tried for treason and hanged? And where was Mackenzie right now? And Lount? And Gibson? And Clancy?

But he was very tired, and this feather bed with the fresh-smelling sheets was so soft. John forgot them all as he drifted swiftly into the best sleep he'd had in a week.

10

More snow had fallen during the night and it was crunching under John's boots as he walked over to the neighbouring farm. Snow clouds were scudding across the sun, sending occasional shadows across the otherwise brilliant day. It almost felt as if life was normal again. Tobias and Bleecker had gone back home. He'd just done the barn chores. It was all back to the familiar routine—except for George missing and a few too many soldiers in the wrong place at the wrong time.

As he came to the split-rail fence in front of the cedar bush that surrounded the Burditts' place, John started feeling nervous. What for, he didn't know. He was just on his way to talk to Nan, and they saw each other all the time.

He took off his cap and smoothed his hair, then changed his mind and put it back on. George, with his clear blue eyes, dark brown wavy hair and lightly tanned skin, could go wherever he wanted and make everybody like him. David Gibson had been an impressive sort, with straight, strong features and his blond hair. Only strange cases like Mackenzie and himself had to put up with flame-coloured mops. That was another odd thing about the little Reformer. If he had to wear a wig, why on earth would he choose red? He could have any colour!

"John! You're back!" Nan came bursting out the kitchen door of the Burditts' large stone house. It was still early, and she hadn't yet changed into her Sunday best. But even her common house attire—a pale beige linen bodice and a brown petticoat—made her look pretty, John thought. Her thick brown hair fell over her shoulders and down her back below her white bonnet.

"We've all been worried to pieces about you," she said. "What happened?"

"Is that young John?" called Mrs. Burditt from just behind her daughter. "Where are your manners, girl? Invite him in."

John stepped inside reluctantly. He had hoped to talk with Nan alone. Now he'd have to listen to Mrs. Burditt. She always knew how to make a short story long.

"Well, John. It's good to see you. It was a terrible time for you and George to be off to Toronto. My, but I would have been worried if I'd been your mother. Two sons right in the middle of it. Of course, your folks were worried when you didn't reach home on Sunday or Monday. We all knew then that something was afoot, since you and George are the last ones who'd skedaddle with their parents' money. Though stranger things have happened."

"Don't even say such a thing, Ma," said the grey-haired Mr. Burditt. He was warming up beside the fireplace after doing the barn chores.

"But by mid-week," Mrs. Burditt went on, "we knew the reason. We heard plenty was going on up there in Toronto, and you *poor* fellows right in the midst of it—"

"Actually, Mrs. Burditt, we weren't," said John firmly. The bustling woman's mouth fell open. It was so rare for someone to manage to interrupt her, and John was usually such a shy, awkward fellow…Momentarily speechless, she ushered him into the big kitchen. They passed the old woodstove near the door and headed over to the long wooden table in the middle of the room. It was covered with a bright, red-checked gingham cloth and there were fresh muffins sitting on a plate in the middle. Nan sat across from John, and beside her sat her ten-year-old brother, Tom.

"Sit down right here," said Mrs. Burditt, bustling again. "I've griddle cakes and piping hot coffee." She handed John a plate of cornmeal griddle cakes and plopped a large empty tin cup on the table in front of him.

Mr. Burditt nodded his head and gave John a welcome smile. "Bet you're glad to be home, son."

"I sure am. It was a long trip—first to Toronto and then on to Belleville with our leftover potatoes."

"For your sister Mary, I reckon. You might have told your parents you were staying to visit. When did you get back?" Mrs. Burditt leaned over John as she filled his cup with coffee.

"Yesterday," he said. "Really late." He stuffed a muffin into his mouth almost whole, so that he could not answer any more questions.

Mrs. Burditt watched proudly as John ate. "I make muffins fresh every morning," she said. "That's just the way my husband likes them. And I always say that a woman should try to please her husband. When I was first married…"

After ten minutes more of Mrs. Burditt talking steadily, John cut in again: "Mrs. Burditt," he began, "could you spare Nan to come over and help mother and Sarah Ann with meals today? Ma's got a terrible headache and Father and Sarah Ann are off to church, and Jane's not there, either. She left early this morning to get her wedding dress fitted at my sister Nancy's. We have soldiers billeted in our sheds, you see, and we have to feed them."

He was getting the hang of it, now—you just broke in and kept on talking.

"Soldiers, billeted here?" Mr. Burditt asked sternly. "It's the first I've heard of it."

"They just came yesterday," said John.

"Well, if she goes," said Mr. Burditt, "I'll take her and fetch her back about the middle of the afternoon."

"Oh, there's no need. I can walk her there and bring her back. Father says the soldiers were mannerly yesterday when they came inside for their meal."

"Nevertheless, I will drive you over in the cutter and have a look around. It being Sunday, I'm not too busy. Tom and I just finished the morning chores."

John almost groaned. When was he ever going to get to speak to Nan alone? Everything he had told them was true, but John had other things up his sleeve as well. Then his stomach clenched. What would they think when they found out George wasn't at home? He decided right then that he'd better confide in Nan and her father, but carefully. Who knew what side they were on?

"Can I go too, Ma?" Tom asked. John frowned at the boy.

"No," said Mrs. Burditt, to John's relief. "I've got errands for you. I need plenty of water from the well. And then you need to dress for church."

"Aww, Ma," protested the boy.

"Do as your mother says," said Mr. Burditt. "I'll be home in plenty of time to drive you."

Shortly afterwards, Nan, Mr. Burditt, and John were sitting all in a row in the cramped seat of the small cutter. When they reached the end of the lane, John turned to Mr. Burditt.

"I've something awful important to tell you, Mr. Burditt, but you can't tell a soul." He looked around at Nan, sitting on the other side of her father. "You too, Nan. No one must know."

"Whatever is it, John?" Nan said, her dark brown eyes wide with curiosity.

"George was detained in Toronto—forcibly. We don't know where he is or what happened to him."

"Oh, no!" moaned Nan. "Poor George!"

What a nice girl she was, John thought, to be so concerned for his brother. He wondered how she would have reacted if he himself had been missing—she'd have fainted, probably.

"So, don't tell anyone," John continued. "If those soldiers hear he disappeared in Toronto during the rebellion, they'll imagine all sorts of things."

"We understand, John. We won't say a word, not even to Nan's mother."

They rode on in silence except for the bells ringing on the horses' harness. A lock of hair fell over John's face. He tucked it under his cap and smiled over at Nan. She was gazing off into the row of pines beside the road and didn't notice.

The little cutter turned off the snow-covered dirt road into the laneway and up the knoll toward the Meyerses house. One of the redcoats strode forward with a loud, "Stop!"

John stared down at him. "I live here," he said. "Why should I stop?"

"Because I said so," the guard flung back.

"On whose authority?" Mr. Burditt asked quietly.

"The authority of the Governor of Upper Canada, Sir Francis Bond Head! We've been told to investigate any suspicious movement in this area."

Father came up the pathway from the barn. "When were you given these orders?" he asked. "Yesterday, I was told you were just passing through on your way to Toronto."

"We got new orders this morning," said the guard.

"From whom?" asked Father. "I saw no one come in!"

"The Belleville militia relayed a message from Toronto. They found the ringleader's carpetbag, containing lists of names. There's a warrant out for all the men on those lists."

"If the rebels had any common sense, they'd head for the States, not come this way," John blurted out. Father looked over at his son and raised one eyebrow.

"Who made you an expert on escape routes?" the soldier asked suspiciously. "Anyway, we aren't looking for the bigwigs like little Mac, just the no-accounts slinking home with their tails between their legs." Then he hesitated, turned to Father, and spoke in a more friendly tone of voice. "Anyway, we've decided to make this here our headquarters, so to speak, while we search the neighbourhood."

"Don't you think you might be needed back in Toronto?" John demanded. "That's where the action is!"

"Oh, really. And how do you know that?"

"This is 1837! It only takes a couple of days to hear about what's going on in Toronto," said Father. "And yesterday was market day in Belleville. There's nothing like a market to spread news around the entire countryside."

"Maybe," said the soldier. He looked at them hard for a while. "We'll be in at noon for our dinner," he said, finally. "Tell the missus we do appreciate her cooking." Father nodded his head but did not smile.

Nan leaned over from the other side of the cutter. "I'd better just run up to the house and get started." She brushed past her father and John along the front of the cutter.

The officer held up his hand to her with a big smile. "May I help you down, miss?" John saw that his dark hair and red uniform made him a dashing sight against the background of the spruce trees and the snow.

"Thank you," said Nan politely. But she did not smile back and barely touched the soldier's hand as her foot reached the round iron foothold on the side of the cutter. Then she leapt to the ground, turned towards the dooryard, ran up the knoll to the front kitchen door, and disappeared inside.

"I'm going to help, too," said John. He hopped down from the cutter and landed on the ground, squarely in front of the soldier.

"Do little boys help with meals around here?" the soldier laughed derisively. "Where I come from, peeling potatoes is penal duty for misbehaviour."

John jammed his cap right down over his forehead and shot a venomous look at the officer, but he caught his father's stern eye and stopped himself. What did he care what the soldier thought, anyway? Helping with this meal was part of his plan—and by the time it was carried out, that soldier would be wishing John had been miles away from the kitchen.

As soon as he had his outdoor things off, John undid his mother's apron and gently pushed her toward the back stairs.

"Mother, you have to get rid of your headache," he said. "Nan and I can take care of things. Don't you worry!"

"Well, if Nan's in charge...I've told her where all the supplies are and be sure not to put too much salt in the potatoes. There's raspberry tarts in the larder and don't forget to add lots of whipped cream."

"Whipped cream! Why are you trying to make them feel so at home, Mother?" John asked, exasperated. "Anyone would think you're a Tory!"

Mother looked steadily at her son. "Soldiers are soldiers, son, and it's better to keep them happy than not. Your Grandpa Meyers was a dyed-in-the-wool Loyalist, and it was British soldiers who were billeted in his home during the War of 1812. But one night they got drunk and beat him and your grandma up. Grandpa recovered fully, but your grandma never got well again. She died only two years later. So know this, son: I'd use up all my cream and every crumb of fruitcake in the house to keep the soldiers from going to the taverns in Trenton or Belleville."

Mother turned and walked slowly up the back stairs.

John stood still, momentarily chastened by his mother's speech. But he wanted the soldiers out, and before George came back. He marched to the potato bin in the pantry and plunged his hands in. "So, here's my plan!" he announced. He hadn't been able to rescue his brother, but he could certainly prevent George being captured again.

"Shhhh, you big, boisterous horse," said Nan, who was already stoking the fire in the woodstove. "You don't want everyone to hear, do you?"

"I'll have to whisper it to you, then," he said. He dumped his armful of potatoes onto the table and ambled over to Nan. When he was finished whispering into her ear, he quickly backed away. The thoughts he was having about that pretty face were making him blush.

Nan closed the stove lid and hung up the poker on the nail.

"Well, I guess we could do it. But who really cares whether the soldiers stay a long time or not? They have to eat somewhere."

Nan and his mother both! They weren't thinking straight.

"Those soldiers are having a holiday at our expense! There's no reason why they shouldn't be marching back to Toronto this very minute."

Nan was washing her hands now. Trying to be as courageous as David Gibson and as quiet and collected as Samuel Lount, he lowered his voice and took what he hoped was a mature tone. "And there's something else, Nan. It's about George." He paused dramatically. "He's somehow involved with the rebels. I'm not sure just how, but that's why he was captured. We think he delivered papers with names from the Midland District to Mackenzie's house."

Nan stopped wiping her hands on the towel and looked up at John with eyes wider than he'd ever seen before.

"Knowing George," John continued, "he'll probably try to escape. And if he's already broken out of jail, he could come walking down our lane any time now. The soldiers will question him, he won't be able to account for his time away, and they'll take him back to jail and slap him with an even heavier penalty."

Nan's face went very red and then very pale. A silence fell heavy between them.

"And then, I'm not exactly out of danger myself. I didn't tell you this before, and you're sworn to absolute secrecy, but—"

"But what, John?"

She was hanging on his every word now. Suddenly he got flustered. "Well, I was captured, too, and made to peel potatoes for the rebel forces…"

Nan looked startled, and then a smile broke out on her face.

John took another tack. "Not only that—I guarded ammunition and hauled in supplies, too. If anyone remembered me by my red hair, for instance…"

Nan tried hard to stifle a laugh but didn't quite succeed.

"Oh, forget it," he said crossly. He sprang up from the couch, walked over to the table, and started peeling potatoes. "Will you go along with my plan or not?"

"Sure, I will," Nan said sweetly to his back. "I…I understand how worried you are about your brother. I'll do my best."

She walked over and put her arm around him for a moment, then went to the other side of the table to continue mixing pie crust. John just about dropped the potato he was peeling. His irritation disappeared and a flush spread over his face.

A twinkle came into Nan's eyes and she leaned over and whispered in John's ear, "I meant to say, 'I'll do my worst'!"

John picked up another potato and started peeling for all he was worth.

11

The smell of roast turkey, frying potatoes, and baking apple pies filled the warm kitchen. John and Nan had been busy for hours now, and had worked themselves into a companionable rhythm. Nan had listened to John tell of his adventures in Toronto with great interest, and now John was sharing some of the stories about little Mac that he'd heard while working in the kitchen of Montgomery's Tavern.

"Mrs. Mackenzie is a clever woman, too," he said, wiping turkey grease on the ruffled apron Nan had made him wear. "I heard someone in Toronto say that some Tory militiamen stormed into her house and demanded to search the place. Mac had files and files of papers that could have been used as evidence against the rebels, so—"

"So she hid them where they could never find them?"

"Well, not exactly. She whispered really loudly to one of her daughters, 'I hope those men don't look in the sheds. I just hope they don't.' The militiamen went there first, of course, and meanwhile her daughter grabbed the files from the *bedroom* and burnt them all in the stove. When those men came in from the sheds and saw the smoke billowing out of Mackenzie's chimneys, they knew they'd been tricked—but there wasn't a thing they could do about it!"

"You sound like you really admire the man, John Meyers. I do believe you are a Reformer!" Nan was only partly teasing.

"No," said John seriously. "I'm not sure the rebellion was a good thing."

"Well, it got lots of attention, anyway," said Nan, whipping up some of Mother's fresh cream.

John thought of the wounded soldier he'd seen, and the buring homes and and fleeing people. "War is ugly, whatever the reason," he said. "Anyway, I'm getting sick of all this rebellion stuff. I'll be glad when George is home." Then, to change the subject, he said, "I have another idea—when school's out this spring, I'm going searching for that Silver Cave."

"It isn't cursed or anything, is it?" asked Nan curiously. "Your brother and your Grandpa Meyers—they both died looking for it, didn't they?"

"Not because of the cave, silly! And I'm sure I can find the place. Especially if…say, Nan, would you…I'd like you to come with me, if you would."

"Perhaps I will, John. I'd like an adventure! Now, let's set the table and get this turkey all carved up. The soldiers are coming for their dinner."

Barking and growls came from the front dooryard.

"Quiet, Boots!" John shouted. He went out to hold the dog as the soldiers filed past, one by one. All of them were staring and smirking as if there was something funny about him. No respect, thought John. And these louts complained about the rebels.

"You look mighty pretty in your mother's apron," said Father, coming up from the barn. He'd gone to check on a sick cow right after church.

John looked down. His face went as red as his hair. There, gracing his hefty chest, were apron ruffles decorated with turkey grease. Nan's fault, he thought, ripping off the apron and trying to stuff it in his back pocket. She should have told him he still had this apron on.

Inside, Nan was standing next to the stove, waiting to serve the men. Sarah Ann had come in from church and had been pressed into service, too.

"We'll be giving thanks for the food, men," said Father, standing behind his chair at the head of the table. "For what we are about to receive," he said, bowing his grey-haired head, "may the Lord make us truly thankful."

John watched the reactions. Two of the men, standing next to Father, bowed their heads respectfully. And three on the side next to the stove crossed themselves. Others smiled derisively as they stared at the girls by the stove, their heads bowed over bowls of food in their arms. The rest just stared blankly at Father with their eyes wide open.

Then Sarah Ann and Nan placed a wooden bowl of soup in front of each man. The men passed around the bread and started tearing up pieces and dropping them into their soup bowls.

Father was the first to splutter. "This soup sure is spicy! Have you any water handy?"

Sarah Ann offered him a big glassful. John glared at Nan, but she wasn't paying any attention. She was supposed to give the bowl with no spices to Father. Where had it gone?

"My soup's fine," said the officer, who was sitting on Father's left. "Guess older men don't like spice anymore. As for me, I love it!"

The soldiers were grimacing, but after their commander's comment, they swallowed in silence.

"I guess I'm used to their mother's cooking," said Father. "Where *is* your mother, Sarah Ann?"

"She has a headache. I hope it doesn't last too long. I'd rather have Mother's food any day—instead of John and Nan's."

The soldiers gave each nervous looks.

"Have some potatoes, men," said Nan. "My first attempt at frying them. We usually serve them mashed at home." Nan and Sarah Ann set down two huge bowls of fried potatoes at opposite ends of the table. "They may be a little overdone," she added apologetically.

The men nodded gratefully, but as the bowl was passed along, only a few took a spoonful. The potatoes were scorched black. Meanwhile, on the other side of the table, the first man scooped out a generous helping and started to eat. "These potatoes are raw, girls! Didn't you cook them?"

Not much, thought John. Everything was going according to plan.

"Well, raw potatoes can't hurt you none," said a young soldier who hadn't eaten anything so far. "Pass 'em along, would you?"

"Careful, they're covered in salt! Got any water, miss?"

"Oh, my, we just ran out," said Sarah Ann. "You know, with the cooking and all. John, get some from the well, will you? And don't forget to wear your boots—it's so muddy right there by the barn."

John opened his mouth to say something, then shut it again. Sarah Ann smiled innocently at her brother. John looked back at her admiringly. Nan must have filled her in.

"The barn?!?!!" one soldier choked out. "You have your well by the barn?"

Father frowned, obviously not favourably impressed by their little ruse. John mosied over to the doorway and began to put on his boots in a leisurely fashion, the better to hear the dinner-table conversation.

"Don't dawdle, boy!" Father snapped at him; then he asked Nan, "Is there any meat?"

John smiled smugly. He and Nan had found a lot of leftover turkey in the cold cellar. They'd recooked it until it was almost dry and hard, and the wings and legs were like rocks. John had torn them loose and then hacked the rest apart and spread the pieces around on one of mother's huge everyday platters.

"I cleaned and baked this turkey all by myself," he heard Nan say as she carried the bird over to the table. "And it's my very first. My mother never let me bake a fowl before." The pride in her voice was unmistakable. "I was pleased to have the chance. But I can tell you," she sighed. "It was an awful job— cleaning out the bird's insides. I never knew that a turkey had so many—well, insides—and that they smelled so *awful!*" John heard the heavy platter clank down on the table. John could picture the men's faces as they stared at the hacked-up mess.

"Is there any gravy to go with this, Nan?" Father barked.

"Yes, there is. I almost forgot." John had seen that greasy gravy. It was full of big blobs of undissolved flour.

"Any more bread?" asked a soldier.

"And butter?" said the one next to him. "We're right out of butter."

"I don't know," said Sarah Ann.

"Get some more butter from the cellar," said Father. "Open a new crock, if need be. And bring up some of your mother's pickles."

"Beets or cucumbers?" Sarah Ann asked.

"What does it matter?" Father said sharply. "Bring both!"

Sarah Ann scurried out the back door and almost fell over John. "I thought you were out at the well," she said.

John shrugged and went to pick up the water pail that people were supposed to leave at the stoop. It wasn't there. He'd have to go get one from the sheds. He ambled toward the sheds, then he heard a noise from beyond the front of the house. He looked to the east end of the dooryard, which paralleled the rutted side road, but all he saw were shadows playing under the grove of spruce trees.

Then Boots barked and started running toward the road. John narrowed his eyes and saw a figure in a brown short-coat turning into the lane. At least it wasn't a soldier. But what stranger would be walking in these parts this close to Christmas? Well, Boots would find out. John shrugged his shoulders and went into the shed.

When he came out again carrying two tin pails, Boots was

wagging his tail and circling around a scruffy man with a bristle-beard.

"John!" the man called, and John dropped the pails on the ground with a terrible clatter.

"George! You've got to get out of here!"

* * *

How did that brother of mine get out of jail? John wondered as he picked up his pails and raced over to the well. There'd be time enough to find out. For now, they must find him another place to hide. John had sent him to the swamp south of the lane, promising to meet his brother there as soon as he could. And it had to be soon, because it was cold, and John had noticed that his brother was limping as he went back down the lane.

John's mind was working so furiously, figuring out where they might hide George, that he forgot about the trick they were playing on the soldiers inside. He hurried up the knoll to the back kitchen door.

"Well, what kept you?" said Father sternly when John stepped inside. The men had finished their meal and were standing now. Everyone turned to stare at John.

"I had to hunt for fresh pails and then wash them out," John stammered. "It took a while."

"Set them on the end of the table, John. And Sarah Ann, where's that dipper?" She handed her father the dipper, and he set it on the water. "Now, help yourselves, men. I'm going to stay and have a talk with my children. Your supper will be better. I promise you!" His voice sounded like steel.

The soldiers took turns drinking the water and smirking at John and the girls, who were staring uneasily at Father's grim face. The men quickly passed on outside.

"You'd better not try this again," said Father. "Hungry men do strange things. I don't know what you thought you would gain by—what is it, John?"

"It's…" John went to the window and pulled the curtain back a little. The men had all gone beyond the dooryard. "It's George," he whispered hoarsely. "He's hiding in the swamp. What are we going to do?"

A silence filled the room. Then Father said, "Well, you'd better take Nan home, John, before her father comes for her. Pick up George on the way. Nan, I know your father will let him stay in the barn for a day or so till we think of something. Just don't tell your mother."

"Oh, Pa won't mind at all," said Nan. Her cheeks were flushed with the excitement. "Isn't it wonderful that George is all right!"

A short time later, John, with Nan tucked in beside him, stopped the single-seat cutter at the foot of the long laneway. George had been watching for them and hurried out from behind a row of cedars. He raced over, jumped right up and into the cutter, and settled down on top of their feet. Nan pulled the buffalo robe off her lap and threw it right over him.

"Thank God, you're safe," she mumbled.

John looked over his shoulder to make sure no redcoats were in sight. Then he flipped the reins lightly on Bonnie. The cutter sped ahead. "So what happened to you in Toronto?" John asked.

George's dark hair, blue eyes, and nose emerged over the edge of the buffalo robe. He looked up at Nan, who smiled sweetly down at him.

"I don't think… "

"Oh, Nan knows everything," said John. "She can be trusted not to tell anyone."

Still, George hesitated. "I was followed…and thrown in jail, just under suspicion. There's no proof."

"But you really were delivering names, weren't you?"

"Something like that, yes." George looked anxiously at Nan.

"Oh, George, I'm on your side! I'd never tell a soul!" she assured him.

"Do Tobias and Bleecker and Father know what you did?" John asked.

"Tobias and Bleecker, yes…but not Father. I didn't want to worry him."

"Well, you worried him anyway. And *me*. How did you break out of jail?"

George frowned. "Well, I told them I only delivered Belleville news for Mackenzie's *Gazette*. No one believed me. I was brought before a committee, and just as they were going to take me back to my cell, Grandpa Meyers' old friend, the Bishop, walked into the meeting. He said they could trust a Meyers' word. A few hours after that I was released. So I guess it was Bishop Strachan who got me off."

"Well, I'm glad for that," said John. "But I could have been killed, you know! Stuck there in the middle of a rebellion that wasn't supposed to happen yet!"

"How did you know that? I thought I told you to go straight home if I didn't meet you at Montgomery's."

"I tried," said John, bitterly. "Then I went hunting for you and after I saw you in that cell at City Hall, I ended up being caught in one of the battles—if that's what you could call it— Mackenzie going nuts riding around in circles on his white pony, the rebels giving up and scattering, all those buildings on fire…For Pete's sake, what was so important about a few scraps of paper?"

John looked down to glare at his brother—and his anger broke like a sheet of ice clattering on frozen ground. George was shaking, in spite of the buffalo robe, and his skin was a ghastly white.

"We need to get you out of the cold," Nan said softly. She reached over and tucked the buffalo robe over George's head. "I'll sneak out some dry clothes and quilts to the hay loft."

John wished he hadn't blown up at George, right in front of Nan. "Anyway, it turned out all right, George. I'm fine now," he said.

"I know. I heard some things about you." George's voice was muffled by the buffalo robe. "I had a chat with Gibson's brother-in-law. You're a brave man, John."

"Can I have that in writing?"

George laughed, and John hurriedly shushed him. They were turning into the Burditt's farmyard.

PART TWO

Rebels in the Family

12

"I don't agree with you, Father," said Tobias. "It was a bloody disgrace about the *Caroline*. Our navy had no business sinking it. It's a wonder we aren't at war with the States."

Wet snow splashed against the windowpanes of the Meyerses kitchen as John sat near the crackling fireplace with Father and his eldest brother. Outside, the mid-February storm piled snow against the rail fences in the frozen fields, but it was warm inside the circle of light cast by the fire. John's eyes were sparkling at the prospect of the debate that was erupting before him. It was Sunday, and Tobias and his wife Elizabeth and their children had dropped by with a huge pan of honey candy. Earlier in the afternoon, Bleecker had appeared after making a house call in Trenton. He'd brought Hanna and their three chil-dren—plus a huge apple-cinnamon pie, the remains of which now lay on the kitchen table. John was surprised they'd gotten this far without politics coming up. Maybe it was in honour of his recent birthday: a few days ago, John had turned sixteen.

At the end of December, the *Caroline*, it seemed, had been taking arms and supplies to Mackenzie and his American followers. They were holed up on Navy Island in the Niagara River, and it was rumoured they were planning to attack Canada. So Colonel Allan MacNab had sent Andrew Drew, the Canadian naval commander, and fifty Canadian volunteers to scuttle the American steamship.

"Well, she should *not* have been taking supplies to Mackenzie," said Father. "Navy Island's right close to Chippawa, on our side. I heard the ship was in Canadian waters when they wrecked it."

"You heard wrong," said Bleecker with his usual confidence. John sometimes thought Bleecker liked correcting everyone else's errors. "They caught the *Caroline* on the American side, docked at Fort Schlosser in New York state. That's where they cut her loose into the Niagara River and set her on fire." He leaned forward. "That makes it an international incident. We could yet see another War of 1812!"

"Nonsense!" exploded Father. "Those…' Patriots', as you call them, are just a few unemployed Americans and a bunch of our own rebels."

"What about Van Rensselaer of Albany? They say he's backing Mackenzie."

"That old aristocrat?" said Father scornfully. "He just doesn't know what to do with his money. Thank goodness President Van Buren has a good grasp of the *real* situation and wants nothing to do with them. He won't even *protect* any Americans caught taking part in an armed invasion of Upper Canada. So we are not going to be at war with the States."

"It's interesting, though, isn't it?" said George. "It seems that Mackenzie intends to do the job right the next time, thanks to reinforcements from the U.S."

John thought it wouldn't take much to improve his last effort. He almost laughed, thinking of all the comings and goings at Montgomery's Tavern. A little organization would do wonders, for a start. Then he grew thoughtful. A lot had happened because of those silly-seeming skirmishes.

"Well, I still say our military had no business taking over an American ship in American waters," said Tobias.

"You're right. And Sir Francis Bond Head had MacNab recalled for doing it," said Father. "But I still say the ship was arming the enemy, and we have a right to protect ourselves."

"Who is 'we'? Protect *what* selves?" asked John suddenly.

Father was so surprised to hear John speak, let alone raise such a strange question, that he didn't know how to respond. But George smiled at John as if he were proud of him. "In a case like this, 'we' usually means government, and 'ourselves' is the people of a nation. But as long as the people are not taken into account in the running of Upper Canada, and 'government' means the Family Compact"—here he looked defiantly at Father—"then Bond Head and MacNab and all the rest are only protecting themselves."

"The sooner Bond Head leaves, the better," Tobias declared. "It's a good thing the British government have called him back, or we'd have kicked him out ourselves, for his lack of action and his arrogant tongue."

"I rather doubt that," said Bleecker quietly. "Nevertheless, the outbreak was bound to come. It is time for a more democratic society in Upper Canada."

"Yes, but we must move slowly," said Father. "Rome wasn't built in a day. We can't change things overnight."

"Sometimes, you have to move fast or go backwards. And Upper Canada has reached that point!" Tobias shouted, striding over to the table and taking up the last mug of apple cider. "I say we should—"

"That's enough, son. I've listened to enough treason for this afternoon." Father got up from his chair beside the fireplace.

"We have a right to express our opinions," said George.

"Yes, in my house, you do. I've raised you this way—always feeling free to say your piece. But these are difficult times. My advice is this: keep your opinions to yourselves when you're out in public. Bishop Strachan may not be around to get you out of jail next time, George!" Father took a deep breath then and said, "I want my children and grandchildren to grow up around me—not banished to some foreign land. Take care. My family is my life. If anything should happen to you…" Father clenched his jaw and stared out into the snowy fields.

Right on time, Tobias's five-year-old son Myron came over with his own news. "Supper!" he shouted.

"Let's go, boys," said Father, taking his grandson's hand and walking up to the kitchen table.

Bowls of creamy mashed potatoes, crispy roast pork, freshly baked buns, and many kinds of pickle had appeared on the kitchen table as the Meyers men were talking. "Help yourselves here, then go find a place to eat in the dining room. We've set up places there," said Mother.

John could see why there wasn't room enough in the kitchen. Jake had arrived with Jane and her new husband, John Wannacott. They must have been there a while, because Jane was helping Mother dish out the food.

Soon they had all found a spot to eat, and arguments about the rebellion were livelier. Jake was the only one who said nothing. He had not decided which side he supported—mostly, John figured, because he'd been occupied taking care of his wife, Eleanor. She'd had their first child last summer and was only now beginning to recover.

"Well, now I suppose we'll get the women's opinions," said Father. "I hope they are like Mother's—against the rebellion."

"Oh, I know the rebels' complaints have some validity," said Mother. "But they must be solved peacefully. I want no more wars in Canada."

Jane chimed in. "I think it's pure treason to rebel against the government. Why, Grandpa Meyers would turn over in his grave if he could hear some of the remarks this afternoon." She poked Tobias in the ribs.

"So you were eavesdropping," said John. "Why didn't you add your bit, then?"

"I most certainly would have, but I was in the middle of icing your birthday cake. For all the thanks I get, I should just take it home and eat it myself!"

"Gee! I didn't know you made it!" said John, glancing over at the dining room table. He had to admit it was huge, and a thing of beauty with its deep whipped-cream icing. Everyone laughed. All John's interest in the discussion had suddenly been blotted out by the delight before him.

"What about you, John?" asked George, addressing Jane's husband.

John thought the man would probably agree with Jane. He

was a mild-mannered clerk, soft-spoken and polite. John knew he had his work cut out for him, having a wife like Jane. She had enough opinions for both of them.

"Jane and I are against any sort of rebellion," said Jane's husband, "but…"

"Stop right there, John," said Jane.

John Wannacott gave his wife a long look and then continued, "…but I do sympathize with some of the rebels' grievances." Jane grimaced, but her husband did not seem to notice.

John scratched his head in amazement. Jane had actually been overruled. So that was the trick. You didn't argue with her. You just kept on talking! Suddenly, John had a new respect for Jane's husband. When he cut the cake and began handing out pieces, John made sure his sister's husband got a large one.

The talk turned to other things for the rest of the afternoon, but later, tramping through the slushy snow on the way to the barn, George said, "Now we can talk without being overheard by the rest of the family."

"What about *this* one?" Tobias punched John playfully in the side of the arm. It was John's turn to do the milking, and his two brothers had volunteered to help.

"Oh, he's all right," said George. "He's on our side."

"This kid is too young to be on *any* side." Tobias sounded serious now.

"He's more mature than he looks," said George. "It's just the freckles and the terrible hair that make him look younger than sixteen."

"George! Don't talk like that about the proud mark of the Meyers family!"

George laughed because Tobias's hair was bright auburn and as curly as John's. Although he was now exactly twice John's age, he had never lost his freckles. The work in the fields on his farm in Sydney Township had made sure of that.

George swung back the heavy wooden door of the cow stable while his brothers stepped inside. John grabbed a pail and stool and began milking, but George stood with his feet apart, rubbed his forehead, and said, "Well, Tobias?"

John milked more slowly so he could eavesdrop better. His brothers were still near the door, so they probably thought he couldn't hear.

"We've got plenty of men from the Midland District, ready and willing to go," Tobias said. "As soon as we've finished the spring seeding."

"You can count me in," said George.

"Fine. I'll find out more next week, after church." Tobias belonged to the Methodist Church. Some folk said that they preached for the rebel cause, but Tobias said they didn't. Still, a lot of Methodists seemed to be rebels.

Just then the wind blew the door open.

"Did you hear footsteps?" said Tobias. He sounded worried.

George did not answer but raced outside to take a look around. He came back in a few minutes. "No sign of anyone. Funny, though; I thought I heard something, too."

"I guess we're just getting jumpy. This old barn has always had creaks and rattles on windy days." They both laughed, but George shut the door tightly and drew the heavy bolt across it. When they resumed talking, John had to strain to hear them.

"Any more news about Lount and Matthews?" George asked.

"They're still in jail. And it doesn't look good," said Tobias. "But there's a petition circulating for clemency. Most people are signing it—folks on both sides, in fact. Sheriff Jarvis claims Lount saved his house from burning when Mackenzie wanted to torch it. The trial won't come until the new lieutenant-governor arrives."

John squeezed harder and pressed his head against the cow's black and white side. In his mind's eye, he could see Lount standing in the front entrance of Sheriff Jarvis's estate, arguing with Mackenzie. Why did Lount have to be the one in jail? He'd saved lives, not taken them. Yet he was the one who was being held. John wondered what had happened to Gibson and Clancy. He stuck his head out from between the Holstein cows. "Hear anything about David Gibson—the one whose house was burned down by the Tories?"

"No one's heard anything definite," said George, "but it's rumoured he may have gone across the border at Niagara."

"Maybe he went with Mackenzie," John said. "We all know he escaped."

"If Gibson made it to the States, he's keeping a low profile," said Tobias. "And so should you, John. You're too young to be in all this."

George looked down at John's curly head and flushed face, more red than usual now. "I think if Gibson had been caught, we would've heard about it before now. In this case, certainly, no news is good news."

"Well, I've got to get to my own chores," said Tobias. "It'll be nice when my sons can help me."

"That'll be a while," George laughed.

"And when are you going to pick out a girl, George? I was married younger than you are now."

"Don't rush me," said George, a smile spreading across his handsome face. "I think I'll wait till all this is over."

"Good idea. At least I know I'll have two single brothers to help Elizabeth out if I was ever caught."

"We won't get caught this time," said George, "but I think Father's right. To be on the safe side, we have to be careful and make sure of our friends."

***

The following Saturday night—February 24—a cold winter storm hurled drifts of snow against the barn's west wall, and the wind howled and whistled all around the brick house on the hill. John checked on the cattle. The Holsteins were a little restless, and the red-and-buff-coloured cats had taken solace on the backs of three of the cows that were lying in their stalls. Boots was curled up in a pile of hay, just in front of the cow mangers. In spite of the wind, the heat from the animals' bodies was keeping the barn warm. John secured the doors and plodded up the knoll to the house, which was now barely visible through the deluge of snow.

As he stepped into the lamp-lit kitchen, he thought about George, still out there in the storm. George always went out on Saturday evenings and usually came back late. Maybe he was courting someone, in spite of his comments in the barn the Sunday before. Or maybe he was visiting Tobias, making plans for whatever they were plotting.

"Goodnight, Mother," he said as he headed towards the drafty stairs. Under the clean, fresh sheets in his feather bed, he lay listening to the howling wind and thinking thoughts of battle and rebellion. Whatever Tobias and George were doing, he planned to get involved, too. He was ready for another adventure. As he drifted happily off to sleep, the grandfather clock in the sitting room struck ten.

John woke suddenly to the sound of loud banging. Maybe the wind had torn the storm door from its hinges, and it was flapping against a door frame. Or had he been dreaming? He turned over.

Then he heard a woman screaming, and more rapping. This was no dream. John jumped out of bed. It was freezing cold, but he was too excited to notice.

Still in his long nightshirt and bare feet, he headed for the back stairway. He crashed into Father at the top of the stairs.

"Come on, son, I might need you," he said.

In the kitchen, his father had pulled back the inside front door and was pushing open the storm door. He held it against the wind, and in staggered Elizabeth with the baby, completely blanketed in her arms. Her two older boys trailed in behind her. Their heads were wound in woollen toques and scarves. Only their red noses and eyes were visible. They looked frightened.

"What is it?" said Father. "What's happened?"

"It's Tobias. They've...taken him. The militia from Belleville."

"They've *what?*" Father exploded.

"The horses," gasped Elizabeth. "The storm was so bad. I just left them loose by the gate."

Father had his trousers and boots on already, so he grabbed

his coat and was gone. John stepped over to close the door, but the wind whipped the outside storm door out of his hands. He had to step onto the snow-packed stoop in his bare feet to pull it closed.

"Come over and stand in front of the oven door, Elizabeth," said Mother. She had followed them down the stairs, and John hadn't even noticed. "There's still a little heat there." She chucked two big pieces of dry wood into the firebox, then turned around and said, "Now let me hold the baby while you get yourself warm. You look half frozen. John, help the boys." She started unwinding the baby from all his blankets and scarves.

"Charles helped Mother drive!" said Myron.

"I had Charles help in case I...well, in case I fainted or something. He knew his way here, and he's pretty good at handling the horses, though he's not even nine yet. Why, he may have to...handle them...from now on!" Then Elizabeth put her head in her hands and broke into shaking sobs.

Father had come in again, and he gave Mother a questioning look. She put her arm around Elizabeth's shoulders. "Please, dear, try to tell us what happened to Tobias."

"They raided some meeting...he was right near the church-yard with a few others...plotting, they said. They brought him home so he could pick up a few things and he told us what had happened. If it had been the military, he wouldn't have been brought home, at all. He would have just disappeared."

Father interrupted. "Well, I know fellows in the Belleville militia. I'll see what I can do."

Elizabeth shook her head. "They're going to hand him over to the military. They say it's treason. He'll be put in jail either in Toronto or in Kingston, I'm not sure which. You might not even be able to find him before he stands trial."

"For what?" Father blustered. "Sure, Tobias speaks his mind—maybe he's said a few things that *sound* treasonous. But he's never *done* anything!"

"Tell *them*," said Elizabeth, "They won't believe me. I know Tobias has taken no action against the government. All he does is talk. Can't a man open his mouth anymore?"

"I'm afraid that's what it's come to," said Father sadly. "I wish my father were alive. He always spoke up for the British, but even he wouldn't put up with things the way they are now."

The grandfather clock struck one. "I'd better get ready," Father said.

"Jacob, you're not striking out in this storm!" Mother's face was very pale in the lamplight.

Father turned to John. "Get your brother," he ordered.

John hurried from the room. George's bed had not been slept in. He hurried back down the stairs.

"Was he at that meeting too?" Meyers looked over at his

daughter-in-law.

"I don't think so."

"I suppose Tobias couldn't say anything with the men watching him."

"Oh, they were friendly enough. I gave them cake and coffee, and they visited while I helped Tobias pack some of his clothes. Tobias could have talked about it in the bedroom if he wanted. He just said that a few of the men from the church were discussing the state of affairs out by the graveyard after the service. Then he told me he was sorry and to tell you in the morning after the storm cleared. But I knew that would be too late."

"We'll go now," Father decided. "Get ready, John."

"But, Jacob…"

Before Father could change his mind, John ran upstairs to get his clothes. He was glad to find his long underwear still warm under the blankets—he always stashed them there so they wouldn't be icy cold in the morning. He found his boots under the end of the bed and then dressed quickly, throwing his nightshirt onto the rumpled quilts.

The wind was lashing pellets of heavy snow against his window. It sounded like a blizzard out there.

13

Bonnie and Duke pulled the sleigh very slowly out the lane in snow already up to their flanks. They struggled through high banks and pulled through deep hollows made by the shifting wind. Father had chosen the sleigh because the cutter would have upset more easily. But even the flat sleigh tipped up and down as the horses ploughed through the heavy, uneven banks of snow. Bonnie and Duke were their most reliable horses—Duke with his extra energy and Bonnie so serene.

Father and John's faces were hidden by lined woollen toques and heavy wool scarves wound round and round their heads. Only their eyes and noses were uncovered. John held the reins tightly, and his father watched the horses' every move, ready to spring into action and take over the reins if John needed help.

Finally, John shouted over the noise of the storm. "Why don't you get warm under the buffalo robes, Father? I can manage the horses. There's no sense in the two of us freezing up here."

"Well…if you can manage. I'll give you a break soon." Father blew out the lantern and tied it to the side of the boxed sled. It wasn't doing much good anyway. Then Father sat upright with his legs and arms crossed and the black buffalo robe wrapped completely around him. He peered out through a narrow parting in the blanket.

"Why are you turning?" Father shouted after a few minutes. He couldn't see far ahead.

"You said you wanted to stop at the Burditts'."

But they were only partway along the Burditts' long lane when Father was over the side of the sleigh and gone. John hopped out, too, to turn the horses and sleigh around. It was a good thing there were trees on either side of the lane—the wind wasn't quite so bad.

The horses could not understand why they were standing still in such weather. They wanted to be on their way to better shelter. John struggled with the reins to hold them steady as he stood there, buffeted by the wind and snow. The ends of his scarves had frozen with the snow, and they whipped icily against his face. He pulled them back and looked towards the house. A low light was flickering from somewhere—probably an upstairs room. That was a good sign.

Maybe it was Nan's room. Maybe it was she who had heard the thumping at the door, who had lit a lantern to go investigate.

He imagined her concern when she saw Father. "Has something happened to John?" she would gasp, and then insist on making him some food for the journey. He imagined her braving the wind and cold so that she could bring it to him herself. She'd see that he was driving, and beg him to be careful. Perhaps she would even—

John was startled out of his exciting thoughts by the sight of Father wading towards him through the drifting snow. His face was grim as he jumped onto the back of the sled and wrapped the heavy buffalo robe around himself. "Let's go!" he shouted. "There's no time to lose."

The wind had been at their backs, but as soon as they reached the main road from Trenton, a bone-chilling blast from the north swept across the fields. It was only five more miles east to Belleville, but Bonnie and Duke had to fight the wind, now, as well as the snow drifts. The cold penetrated through John's gloves, leaving his hands stiff and almost numb. But he kept holding onto the reins and tried to turn his face towards the south. The left side of his face was starting to go numb and the clumps of frozen snow were scratchy.

Just as he was thinking he might collapse, John heard Father clambering up to the front of the sleigh. "I'll take the reins," he said. John was too frozen to say a word. He dropped the lines, climbed onto the floor of the sleigh box behind Father, and pulled the buffalo robe around himself. He couldn't stop shaking.

"We're three-quarters there," shouted Father, and then a beautiful silence fell. They had entered an uncleared lot that stood on the road between Belleville and Trenton, a government grant to a member of the Family Compact who had no interest in farming it. The noise of the storm was softened by the woodland, though the wind still howled in the distance beyond the woods.

The horses plodded along slowly. The road was only a trail here, narrow and uneven. Then, without warning, the horses came to a dead stop.

"What's the matter?" John gasped.

"Nothing. I stopped the horses. They need a rest and it's more sheltered here." Father bent down next to John and threw the other robe around his own shoulders. He still held the reins tightly.

About ten minutes later, Father jumped up. "Giddap," he said. The horses had now caught their breath, and they struggled on without a murmur.

"I can drive again," John offered, but Father shook his head.

Two hours later, they came plodding down the snow-laden hill and into Belleville. They rode close past the windy southern bay on their right.

John looked across at the shortest space to the peninsula on the other side of the bay. That was the spot where his Aunt Mary had begun the ferry service to Prince Edward County—after her first husband had died and before John was born. A young widow, she soon married again and kept expanding her ferry business. But all the boats were in shipyards for the winter. They weren't needed because sleighs rode freely across the cold, frozen wasteland of ice and snow.

Finally, they crossed the narrow, frozen Moira River near the place where it joined the bay and entered a neighbourhood of silent streets, piled high with drifting snow. There were no lights in the windows. It was probably about six o'clock, but John could not be sure.

Then, they found Jane's street and turned into her laneway. Father drove the horses right into the shed behind the house and tied them up securely. John brushed Duke and Bonnie, then shook the buffalo robes and laid them over their backs. The horses snorted and stomped and nosed happily into the oats John poured into the trough.

Father headed for the back door and knocked loudly. As John came up close behind him, one of the upstairs windows suddenly glowed with light.

***

"I can't understand why you're holding my son. Surely, you

know that he's no more guilty of treason than I am." Just inside the Belleville jail, John was standing to the side while Father leaned over the jailer's wooden desk. The bare grey limestone walls of the jail made John shiver.

The jailer laid down his quill pen and looked up sadly into Father's face. "I don't doubt that, Jacob," he said quietly. "But the Toronto soldiers will do as they please. It seems that your son was overheard making plans—war plans—with two other men."

"Oh, I know he's been saying enough," said Father. "But that's the way young men are these days, and it means nothing. It's all hot air. Surely, you can't jail a man for that."

"I'm afraid so."

"But it's *actions* that get a man caught for treason. Words aren't anything."

"He'll have his day in court. He can explain all that."

Father tried another tack. "He's been in the Midland District the entire autumn and winter. No uprisings happened here."

"The men didn't say he was involved in an uprising. They just said he may be planning—" The man stopped himself. "I'm sorry, Jacob, I can't tell you what they said." He lowered his voice and leaned forward. "I'm not supposed to do this. But why don't you talk to him yourself?"

"Thank you. I'll do that," said Father.

John watched Father disappear down the dark, narrow hallway behind the jailer's desk. Then he turned to gaze out the still, dim street. The storm seemed to be easing up.

Father and the jailer were back soon. "Thank you," said Father again, as they passed through the doorway and down the stone steps to the street. Father's shoulder's drooped, and his face was grey with fatigue. John suddenly knew his father was growing old. Well, he was sixty-one, after all—but still, it gave John a frightened feeling.

"Remember when I was in the militia?" Father asked, as they trudged through the snow.

John did. Father used to go away with them a lot. When he did, Mother used to say he was "going on a spree." She never sounded too happy about being left with the boys to manage all by themselves.

"Well, I'm going to see the captain of my old militia unit," said Father as he and John walked to the sleigh. "Jones replaced me. I'll see if anything can be done from that angle."

So, Father wasn't ready to give up, after all. He took the reins and drove the struggling horses up the short hill on Bridge Street, drawing to a halt in front of a stone cottage. He handed the reins to John, walked up the front steps and knocked, then disappeared inside.

The rawness of the storm had passed, but a deeper cold had set in. John tied Duke and Bonnie to the hitching post in front of the house. He stomped his feet in the snow a few times to warm them, then got back into the sled, huddled under one of the buffalo robes, and waited for Father.

Soon the clouds parted, and the sun shone upon a world of fresh whiteness. A milkman was delivering late. The snow had probably held him up. His single dapple-grey horse plodded along the street from house to house. John watched and wondered who was milking their cows back on the farm. Was George at home, or had something happened to him, too? John sighed. Ever since that fateful market day in Toronto, he seemed destined to rescue one or the other of his brothers. When would this whole rebellion mess be over? When they were all in jail?

When spring came, John vowed, he would talk to Nan about the Silver Cave again, and they'd go looking for it. He was sure she would come. For one thing, she liked him. She was always asking him to tell about his week in Toronto, and congratulating him again on his cleverness in keeping George from being recaptured. She was adventurous, unlike most girls. That was one of the things John liked about her.

Once again, thoughts of Nan were interrupted by the arrival of his father. One look at Father's face told John more than he wanted to know. "No news?" he asked.

"Not now." Father settled himself in the seat beside John.

"The Captain doesn't hold out much hope. Though he treated me fine—and Tobias, too, for that matter. But he doesn't know if Tobias will be taken to Toronto or to the Kingston jail. Kingston would be better—he wouldn't be classed with the Toronto rebels. I don't want him tried with those fellows."

"When will we know where they're going to take him?"

"I don't know," said Father, "but drop me at the jail." The snow on the streets was packed down now from the weight of all the sleighs on the road. One man perched up on a high seat at the front of his sleigh waved at them. Father returned the salute as though nothing was wrong.

John stopped in front of the jail and Father jumped down from the sleigh. "Go back to your sister's," he said. "Water the horses, then get some sleep. Meet me back here in the middle of the afternoon. You'll need to go back home then, to see how they're doing with the farm chores."

"Won't you be coming?"

"I don't know yet. I'll tell you when we meet."

No sooner had John removed his snowy outdoors clothes than Jane had him seated in front of a plate heaped with fried pork, warmed-up potatoes rolling in butter, and toast with wild strawberry jam. He'd eaten a few cold biscuits with Father when they first arrived, but that didn't impede his appetite any. He washed it all down with a mugful of fresh, cold milk from the milk sleigh. Jane always had been a good cook. He hadn't really thought about that before now.

Jane was strangely quiet, and when he had finished eating, she led him to their spare bed. He took off his boots and dropped into it. "Things will be all right, John," said Jane. She reached into a large cedar chest and took out two more quilts, spreading them out over the others already on top of John. "Father can take care of Tobias."

John was surprised. He had expected her to rave about Tobias's stupidity and foolhardiness. Instead, she was actually being kind. His sister had changed since she married John Wannacott, he thought.

It seemed he'd only just lain down when his Father was shaking his shoulder saying, "John, John, we have to go now."

John opened his eyes and stared up at his Father. "Why...where?" Then it all came flooding back to him. "How did you get here?"

"I walked. It wasn't far. C'mon, now. I want to get back before dark."

"What about Tobias?"

Father's voice was flat and despairing. "They're taking him to Toronto."

14

A week passed. At the Meyers home everyone was worried, even Father, though he spoke of friends in Toronto and the surety of Tobias's getting off. There were the extra chores for John and George, as well, for they were doing all Tobias's milking as top of their own, and mucking out the stables and everything else that required a man's hand on an Ontario farm.

So when Saturday night rolled around, and with it, an invitation to a skating party at the Burditts', John wasn't sure he was up to it. George wasn't around, as usual—he did most of the work at Tobias's farm, and Sundays he usually dressed up and went out, who knows where—and John didn't relish the thought of the long, cold trek there and back alone. Only the thought of Nan being there made John willing to set out after supper into the deep cold. Burditt's pond was the best place to skate in the neighbourhood. The water wasn't deep, but it made smooth ice—and the young people in the area kept the surface cleared.

There would be hot cider in a kettle above the pondside fire, and afterwards the Burditts usually invited everyone in for tea. Neighbour girls took turns bringing their own popcorn, cookies, cake, and maple sugar candy.

The moon was full and its reflected light on the fresh white snow illuminated the whole area almost as brightly as the sun. John stood a moment and watched Nan circle in and out among the other skaters, more graceful than anyone. Her thick brown hair streamed out below her red toque with the tassel bobbing on top. Her close-knit red coat was fitted to her waist, and her dark navy trousers bagged a little because they'd belonged to her older brother, who was now married and living away from home. A lot of girls wore their brothers' hand-me-downs at times like this—but Nan managed to look good in them.

John guessed he'd better get out there and skate, too. Once more fellows arrived, Nan wouldn't be skating alone! He grabbed his skates and started to tie the wooden base to his boots. He wrapped the leather thongs around them and, for extra security, made a twist around each ankle.

Then he jumped up and started thumping through the snow, down the knoll towards the pond. Suddenly, his foot caught on something under the snow, and he flew forward, landing on his right knee and arm.

"Yeow," John yelled. He turned around, and sure enough the

corner of a log was sticking through the snow. He had a notion to kick it but didn't. His knee hurt too much. Stupid log, he fumed. He stifled a torrent of words, brushed the snow off his legs and back, and ambled slowly on down to the edge of the ice. From there, he tried to spot Nan again in the crowd of about twenty skaters who were circling around the pond. She was just emerging, so he stepped out on the ice and waved briskly. She saw him and started over his way. Her eyes seemed to be sparkling. John glided the few strokes back to her and slipped his arm under hers. She smiled up at him warmly and they skated forward together, whirling in and out among the others without actually seeing them. She was a strong skater, John remembered. But this was the first year they'd actually skated arm in arm. He liked how it felt.

"Do you remember, John, how we used to race each other around this pond?" asked Nan.

John smiled. He sure did remember.

"Like to try it again?" she asked.

"Just as soon not. More folks are coming. We might run into someone."

"That never used to worry you. Remember that time you piled right into your brother Bleecker and knocked him over?"

John remembered. Bleecker had been trying to make an impression on Hanna, now his wife; he had been furious with

John, not because Bleecker had had the wind knocked out of him, but because he'd been made to look foolish. Now, for the first time, John felt a bit of sympathy for his solemn elder brother.

"I was just a kid then," he told Nan.

She looked at him, wide-eyed. "Why, John Meyers, you're only fifteen now!"

"Sixteen," John corrected her.

"That's right! I forgot you had a birthday. But still, you're hardly a man." She laughed merrily.

John's face burned. They were the same age, for Heaven's sake! Yet here she was, basically calling him a little boy.

"I'm five foot nine, I'll have you know," he pointed out, in what he hoped was a dignified tone, "and Father says I'll be over six feet in no time."

Nan giggled. "Well, I'd better race you now, then. If those legs get longer, I won't have a chance." She let go of his hand, pulled her arm free, and was gone. Then, over her shoulder, she shouted, "Meet you back at the bonfire."

In spite of himself, John rose to the bait. Bent over almost double, he sped out in long strides. She kept ahead of him for a while, but he soon reached her and then went sailing by. Her musical laugh blended into the other sounds. He circled around and back to the side of the ice nearest to the bonfire where he waited only about a minute before she skated over to him—in fact, she almost fell on him. He reached out and caught her.

"Thanks," she laughed, grasping him around the waist. "Whoosh, I was going too fast—for me." John dropped his arms clumsily and flushed a little.

Together, they climbed up the knoll to the logs set out around the fire. He threw on another chunk of wood and sat down.

"You can still outrace me, John," said Nan, smiling up into his face. "But I think one of the reasons I'm a pretty good skater today is that I was always trying to beat you."

John beamed at her. Nan took off her red woollen mitts, laid them on one knee, and held out her hands towards the fire. "I wonder how much more skating there'll be this winter."

"Maybe no more and maybe another month," said John, studying the fire intently as it burst into fresh flames. "Weather can change suddenly in March."

"Did you find Tobias yet?" Nan asked without warning,

John evaded the question. "How do you know about that?" he asked in turn.

"I was listening on the stairs the night of the storm. When your father came, I was afraid...well, anyway, there are all kinds of rumours."

Nan had been afraid...for him! Flooded with warm feeling,

John decided he'd share what he knew. He didn't want to worry her, so he finished by telling her a little about Father's plans. "He has friends in Toronto, and he's sure he can get Tobias free. Tobias had nothing to do with the skirmishes in Toronto. He was here in Sydney Township the whole time. Father believes in the British system. He feels he can persuade the authorities that in Upper Canada, a man can't be condemned simply for voicing an unpopular opinion."

"Still, your sister-in-law must be frantic. I'll go over tomorrow and see if I can help with the children."

Eagerly, John asked, "Do you want me to take you over?"

"I think Mother'll want to help, too. Pa will take us."

Now John wished he hadn't said anything—it would all be going straight to Mrs. Burditt's ears. Well, he couldn't worry about that. He was just going to enjoy skating.

"Let's go back on the ice," he said. "It's such a bright night for it."

"Sure." Nan jumped to her feet. It seemed they were thinking alike.

As they started walking slowly down the hill through the snow, she pushed her small hand into his. He held onto her hand and squeezed it gently. Then, looking down at her, John watched her turn her face up and smile at him. It was a good thing the moonlight wasn't quite as bright as the sun. If it was daytime, Nan would have seen he was blushing.

"In the spring," he said, "let's head out together and find the Silver Cave. Do you think you could get away?"

"That would be an adventure all right. Maybe some day, we'll go hunting for it."

At the edge of the ice, John took Nan's arm and they sped around the pond. After they'd raced around for about twenty minutes, John slowed down a bit, and Nan fell into line with him. They were going more and more slowly now—sort of like some of the older couples. John didn't mind at all. He pulled Nan a little closer.

Then, not fifteen feet away, he saw George swing out from behind another skating pair. At that moment, Nan stumbled.

"I think I need to rest a bit," said Nan. "Why don't you go get some cider?"

John wasn't in the mood for cider, but he went. While it was being ladled up out of the steaming kettle, he saw George skate up to the log where Nan was sitting and offer her his arm. Together, they glided off. George did have his nerve. Why was he skating with Nan? Couldn't he pick a girl his own age? He'd give them a few rounds, and then he'd step in.

He waited, shivering, at the edge of the ice. At last George and Nan circled closer to him, slowing down. Then a fellow from Trenton in a fancy dress-up suit skated in front of John to tap George on the shoulder.

Oh, no, thought John. Another one before me. But the Trenton fellow was out of luck.

"You're no sport, George Meyers," he said as George and Nan skated away, still arm in arm.

John went back to the fire to warm up. Opposite him across the flames he spotted the new schoolteacher, Miss Hildreth. She'd come up from New York in January because the last schoolteacher had left to get married.

Maybe he should ask *her* to skate. Mother had always told him to be polite to older women. Besides, he felt sorry for her sometimes, the way the older boys acted in class. This was her first school, and she was having a hard time controlling them. He bet she'd be glad when spring came and they were kept home to help on the land.

John skated over towards Miss Hildreth. "Good evening, ma'am, may I have the privilege…?" he asked quietly.

"I'd like that, John Meyers," she said briskly. John took her hand and tucked it around his arm, and they pushed smoothly off.

"So you folks skate in New York, too, do you?" John asked.

"I skated a lot back home," she said. "Let's go faster."

"Sure," said John, gulping. He didn't think that would be such a good idea. Unlike Nan in her borrowed trousers, Miss

Hildrith was wearing a very stylish, flowing skirt. He was afraid he might trip over it. Then he'd be in trouble at school. The joke would last till the summer break.

As if she had read his thoughts, she added, "If we went faster, my skirt would fly back, out of the way of our skates."

John gulped again. She was looking at him, waiting. Oh, well, there was nothing to do but speed things up.

"See, it's easier," she said. And it was easier. They were gaining momentum and sailing around now almost as fast as he and Nan had gone. Miss Hildreth was not a bad skater for an older woman. And come to think of it, she didn't look so old out here on the ice. In fact, she looked completely different than she did in school. Her stern schoolteacher face was gone, replaced by a wide smile and sparkling eyes, and her dark hair, normally tied under her bonnet, surrounded her face with soft curls that glistened in the moonlight.

"You're a great skater, John," said Miss Hildreth. "Let's really speed now!" This time, John did not hesitate. They went whirling in and out and cut right in front of Nan and George. Let George watch *him*, now, sailing over the ice with a fashionable New York lady!

Just as John was launching into a really good show-off act, a whistle sounded and they all stopped. "Let's head back to the house, now," said Mr. Burditt, the "official" chaperone.

Everyone skated over to the sides to take their skates off their boots. "Thank you, John, for the skate," said Miss Hildreth. "It was lovely." John nodded and smiled. His teacher was very pretty, he decided. And she wasn't so old, after all—just turned seventeen, John had heard his mother say.

Then a pompous man, who must have been thirty-five if he was a day, marched up beside them. "Well, there you are, Louise," he said, ignoring John. "I thought I'd lost you." She gave John a last smile, then took the man's arm and skated away.

"Now, who was *that?*" thought John. It seemed to be his day for losing skating partners.

As soon as John had his skates off he went to find Nan.

"You're coming up to the house, aren't you, John?" she asked.

"Of course. I wouldn't miss it," he said enthusiastically. Daringly, he offered her his arm. They weren't skating now, but maybe… To his delight, she tucked her hand into the crook of his elbow, and they set off up the slope towards the house.

But then George stepped up on the other side of Nan. "Well, I think I'll join my little brother and his best friend," he teased.

"Aren't I a lucky lady!" Nan laughed. "*Two* Meyers boys to help me along!" She put her other arm through George's.

John scowled. Though Nan's chatter included them both, he was silent all the way up to the house.

15

A couple of weeks after the skating party, there was Sunday dinner at Jacob Meyers', and the whole family came—except Tobias,
of course. All during dinner, talk was of Tobias and the upcom-
ing trial in Toronto. Elizabeth looked exhausted. She had plenty
of help, but constant worry had drawn lines in her face that
hadn't been there before. John had found himself thinking of
another face—Mrs. Gibson's, white with horror on the way to
her sister's, with her house in flames behind her. It seemed
unfair that women like Mrs. Gibson and now Elizabeth had to
suffer the consequences of their husbands' actions.

The meal over, the men gathered in the other room to talk
while the women started to clear the table.

"You know," George said, "we have a new calf and I'm going
down to check on it. Anyone want to come along?"

The women looked resignedly at one another as all the
brothers quickly jumped to their feet, grabbed their coats off the

chair by the door, and followed George outside. Unfortunately, John was last in the line, and Jane grabbed him by the arm. "Not so fast, young man; you're too young to join the men for a nip. And anyway, we need you to run a few errands."

"That's right, John," Mother said. "Just wait a bit and I'll have these leftovers ready for the pigs."

John pulled on his rough coat and sat on the chair by the door. He swung a leg back and forth and watched as the women talked and worked and his father dozed in his armchair by the fire. He knew he was missing more than a nip of hard cider— they'd be talking politics, and he'd like to catch up on all the news about his rebel friends.

Finally, Mother handed George a full bucket of slops for the pigs. "Now, John, I may need you for something else. Don't dawdle too long giving this to the pigs."

John whipped the bucket out of Mother's hand and was out the door in a flash. He dumped the bucketful of slops into the pigs' trough and hurried over to the barn door to peek in, guessing that if he just walked in, his older brothers would throw him out again. There was a balmy feeling in the air—as if the piles and drifts of winter snow would start melting soon and spring might actually come again. Sunlight streaked through cracks in the barn walls and across the upper haymow that circled around the inside of the barn.

"…make our move," George was saying. "We're taking the *Sir Robert Peel* to replace the *Caroline*. It's a Canadian ship, owned by men in Brockville, and it delivers produce between Kingston and Prescott. It picks up passengers from the States, too."

"I'll have no part of that!" said Jake.

"Well, I will," said Bleecker. "It's not at all as if we were going into battle."

John was a little surprised at Bleecker's quick response. So far, he'd supported the rebellion in thought and attitude only.

"How can you capture a ship without a battle?" asked Jake. "You fellows are dreamers!"

"We have it all planned," answered George. "We'll sneak onto the ship real quietly when they're taking on fuel at Wellesley Island, and capture the crew. They'll come to no harm—we'll let them off on the Canadian side."

"And the first thing they'll do is run to Fort Henry," said Jake. "Before you know it, there'll be soldiers after you."

"But by then, we'll be in the United States," said George.

"And you wouldn't be allowed back! What would be the good of that?" asked Jake.

John heard some movement and peeked in further, so that he could see them all. Jake was leaning against the side of Father's best cutter, the two-seater. "How much of all this does Father know?" he asked.

George slowly drew a long piece of hay between his perfect teeth. "You'd have to ask John—he's home more than I am these days," said George. Then he looked straight in John's direction. John stepped back a little—and bumped right into his father. Father shook his head at his youngest son, but he was smiling. He strode into the barn, and John was right on his heels.

"I have an inkling about what you boys might be getting up to," said Father soberly. Bleecker, Jake, and George exchanged glances. "But I don't want to know for sure. And I don't want anyone else to know, either—especially the womenfolk. So, if you must talk, keep it quiet. Tobias had a bigger mouth than he should have had in these times. I expect you boys to be wiser than that. Understand? Having the military nosing around here is the last thing I want. See that you give them no cause to."

"Yes, Father." It was Bleecker who spoke, and John was surprised at the meekness of his tone.

Meyers smiled. "And you might want to find another place to talk—or at least post Boots as sentry. It's as easy for military spies to listen at doors as it is for younger brothers." Father turned and left the barn amid whoops of laughter.

"Let's get back to business, then," said George, taking charge.

"What about John?" said Jake. "This is no business for womenfolk *or* children."

"I've seen more action than you have, Jake! Or you,

Bleecker!" John said. He was still smarting from that crack of
Father's, and he was darned if he was going to let his brothers
gang up on him.

"John's no pipsqueak," said George; but before John could
feel grateful, his infuriating brother added, "Why, only last night
he was skating with the schoolteacher, and surely that's man's
work."

Again the barn rafters rang with laughter. John's ears
burned—but he didn't leave. And soon, the brothers were giving
George their full attention again.

"We won't wait to be 'allowed' back from the States," said
George. "We'll march back with Mackenzie and his army to
liberate all of you."

"Well, I for one won't go along with this plan. Eleanor's
unwell, and I'll not leave her," said Jake.

"Most of the men have young families. Lount has six children and Matthews has eight, not including his two stepchil-
dren," said Bleecker. "So that's no reason to hang back. Count
me in!"

"What about your patients?" asked Jake.

"They can manage without me for a few days. So many
of them are suffering unnecessarily from this recession and
overwork. I'll be helping them in the long run by supporting
the rebels."

"What if you're caught?" asked Jake, placing a hand on Bleecker's shoulder. "What about Hanna?" Bleecker's wife was expecting a baby in the summer.

"You don't have to come all the way, Bleecker," said George. "A lot of fellows are coming only as far as the ship."

After a while, Bleecker nodded. John thought he looked relieved. "The conquering army might need a doctor. I'll be waiting for you."

"You're talking theft and treason," said Jake. He was his father's namesake in more than name.

George laughed. "Most of the young men of the Midland District are in on this. The jails are full now—where would they put us?"

"What of our farms? Spring's our busiest time!"

"After the seeding's done, I'll simply plan a business trip to Kingston. That's all Father will know. And John will still be here."

It was definitely John's turn to speak up, now. "I will *not* be here," he said. "I wouldn't miss this for the world." He didn't care what Father had said. This sounded like a bigger adventure than the Toronto trip!

All the brothers looked at John in consternation.

"I'm sixteen years old!" he said.

"Look at what you've done, George," said Jake. "We've got a young rebel on our hands."

"He *has* seen more action than you have. When he went to Toronto…"

"Tall tales," said Jake scornfully. "He was always a kid who could dream up stories to fit any occasion."

"Yes," Bleecker added. "I heard the real story—they found him after the Toronto battles, buried in the mud on Yonge Street. A good hiding place!"

George shook his head. "Well, I don't know who you've been listening to, because I heard he—"

John was sick of them talking like he wasn't even in the room. "I can fight my own battles, thank you," he told George coldly. "And yours, too. Who kept you from being recaptured the moment you got home from Toronto?"

The sudden silence was broken by a baby's cry in the yard.

"Well, it's getting close to suppertime. Let's go in," said George.

And nothing more was said about rebellion that day— Upper Canada's, or John's.

PART THREE

Rebel's Reward

16

"I got you into enough trouble before," said George. "You cannot go this time!"

As usual, George thought he was looking out for his younger brother, but he was actually infuriating him to the core. It was Sunday the twenty-seventh of May and the plan to capture the *Sir Robert Peel* was about to be launched. John had begged off going to church by claiming he had a toothache—and now George was keeping him from his one opportunity to get to Kingston for the start of the action.

"Besides," George went on, "there's no room. I'm getting a ride to Casey's place and they can't take any more."

"I'll walk," said John stubbornly.

"To Napanee? You'll never make it by noon tomorrow."

"Go, then. Just don't expect me to come running to your rescue when you're caught this time!"

John turned away in a huff, and Boots jumped up to lick his

hand. The air was heavy with the rich fragrance of lilacs—white along the south side of the path and deep purple next to the house. A robin half-hidden between the white blossoms whistled from its perch, and a brown wren chirped loudly beside the house. A gentle breeze from the south ruffled John's red hair and would have lifted his spirits if George hadn't so thoroughly dampened them. He had to figure out some other way to get to Kingston, if he couldn't ride with the others to Napanee.

John leaned against the top rail of the fence that divided the dooryard from the pasture and looked down the hilly knoll to the swamp just back of their house. A golden haze of cowslips was sprouting up on the edge of the marsh, but John didn't see them. He was too busy thinking about his predicament. It wasn't fair that he was being left behind. After all, the planting was done, and Father could easily keep up with the chores.

Father wasn't nearly so strained as he had been, now that his worry about Tobias had eased somewhat. He hadn't been shipped to Toronto, after all, as Father found out when he went there. Tobias had been accused of plotting against the government, but the spies hadn't been government men at all, merely local tramps looking for a fast handout. One of them had probably heard Tobias and George talking in the barn, then brought a gang with him to the Methodist Church graveyard that fateful night. Father felt confident of his chances in court against the word of a couple of tramps, but to be on the safe side, he was trying to get a smart, new lawyer in Kingston to take the case. When John had heard the lawyer's name, he'd nearly choked. It was John A. Macdonald. John vowed to himself never to meet the man face to face. If he was recognized, the fact that he'd been in Toronto during the skirmishes wouldn't help Tobias one bit.

John felt someone jump up on the rail fence beside him. It was Nan.

"Why so sober, John?" she asked.

"George is leaving for Napanee, and he won't let me go," said John. A few weeks before, John and Nan had talked about the planned raid, but since then John had been home from school to help with the spring planting. So he supposed that Nan had forgotten all about their chat.

"I thought so," said Nan. "Well, you'll cheer up when you hear my news. I've arranged a ride to Napanee."

John's mouth fell open, then he stuttered, "How—? When—?"

Nan laughed. "Oh, John, you do look funny! Last evening I was over watching Elizabeth's children while she was out. George came inside when he finished the chores, and we got to talking. Well, the long and short of it is that I've got us a ride."

John narrowed his eyes at her. "What do you mean, 'us'? What on earth is going on in your mind, Nan Burditt?" He had always known that Nan was more adventurous than most girls, but was she actually planning to…?

"The Browns—my great-aunt Eliza and her husband—have grain to sell, and there's likely more cash in Napanee than here, it being so close to Kingston. Besides, Great-aunt Eliza wants to visit her sister-in-law in Napanee for a few days. They've arranged for their neighbours to do their chores," Nan explained, "but Ma is worried about them going alone in case one of them gets sick on the way." Nan jumped down from the top fence rail. "Pa's oldest sister, who's widowed now, lives in Napanee. I'll stay there while Great-aunt Eliza is visiting with her sister-in-law. That's her first husband's sister, and Ma says she's always been a crabby one. She bets they'll start back home in a few days."

"And just how did you find out about all this?" John was staring at Nan in amazement.

"Well, Ma's always sending me over to Great-aunt Eliza's with a bit of baking, and Pa keeps checking in on them. Ma says, 'They're kin, and folks always watch out for kin.' So, what are you waiting for? Get going!"

"Wait a minute—why didn't your father bring you today?" John was having his suspicions about Nan's tale. "Are you sure your parents know about me coming along?"

"Of course they do, silly. I suggested you come along to help with the driving. Mr. Brown is seventy-eight now, and Great-aunt Eliza never did take to handling horses even when she was young."

"And your father agreed, just like that?"

"Well, they agreed to the part about me going along a while back, but then Pa just found out last night that they planned to leave today, and he's busy with a sick cow. So you're an answer to prayer as far as he's concerned."

Boots nosed his way between them as they talked. John reached down and stroked the dog's thick golden coat of hair. "Sorry, Boots, you won't be able to come along." To Nan he said, "Thanks, Nan. This sounds like a great plan."

"Yes, isn't it?" Nan grinned.

John grinned back. There sure weren't too many like Nan Burditt. Most girls wanted to stay home and learn how to cook, sew, clean house, milk cows, and work in their gardens. Nan knew how to do all those things, but she wanted more, too.

"Now go pack your bag," she told him. "Keep it light but bring as much food as you can."

"Yes, and a compass and a few other supplies."

"Why, John Meyers, are you planning on getting lost?" Nan said in mock alarm.

***

All the time he was getting ready, John's spirits rose. He hid his bag of supplies in the bushes by the drive, and later told George he was heading over to see Elizabeth. He'd left a note pinned to his mother's nightdress, so they wouldn't know where he'd gone until after George left. George sure would be surprised when John showed up! But before that, there would be the pleasure of the journey, with Nan at his side. Just the two of them!

Well, almost. Nan was told to sit on the grain bags, while Mr. Brown made John sit up front, "so you can watch how these horses handle"—as if John were six instead of sixteen. When John finally took the reins, Mr. Brown wanted to stay up front to keep an eye out.

"Don't let the reins get too slack, there, son," the old man said.

John doubted the horses were likely to startle, much less run away. He sighed. "Sir, I drove our team all the way back from Toronto by myself," he said.

"You don't say!" said Mr. Brown. "Where was George?"

John realized he'd said too much. "Oh, George was… Well, you see there were these robbers…"

"Yes, I do remember now, hearing a little about that. I don't want the womenfolk worrying. Not another word."

John was glad to oblige. He had no desire to retell *that* tale. To explain George's late return last December, Father had told everyone that robbers had attacked them; John had bolted with the team and wagon, he said, but George had secretly followed the robbers until he was able to recover their market money. Besides being a lie, the tale made John look like a coward. Father should have been able to think up a better story than that!

After a while, though, Mr. Brown started dozing off, so Mrs. Brown made him a bed in the wagon box beside her. Nan climbed forward and John sat up straighter. At last! John spoke to the horses and they picked up the pace a little. Over the next couple of hours, John couldn't decide which he liked better— Nan's bright voice, or the companionable silence they fell into between conversations. Then the silences grew longer, and Nan began to doze, her head falling against John's shoulder.

It was nearly midnight when they approached Napanee. John shook his shoulder a little to rouse Nan.

"Nan. Nan, do you want me to bring you to your aunt's now?"

Nan yawned. "What's that, John?" Her hair was rumpled where it had rubbed on John's sleeve.

"Is your aunt expecting you tonight or tomorrow?" John asked.

"Neither, really." Nan yawned again. "Ma only posted the letter a while ago. Aunt Bea won't get it until Friday, and by that time I'll be there." She gave him a sideways look. "Why, I could go along with you and no one would be the wiser!"

"Nan Burditt, what is going on in your mind?"

Nan lowered her eyes. "I just can't stand the thought of sitting around worrying instead of going out and doing something useful." She looked up at him again. "The Meyers boys need a proper farewell, and I'm sure there's something for women to do before a battle. Isn't there?"

"Well, women do follow soldiers in battle sometimes and do the housekeeping," said John. "But I didn't see any women at Montgomery's Tavern. I had to do the women's work."

"Well, I brought along some boy's clothes, just in case," said Nan. "If necessary, I'll go at it like Joan of Arc—dressed like a soldier!"

"She was burned at the stake!"

"I don't intend to be discovered," said Nan firmly. "Besides, that isn't done anymore."

"Hanging kills you just the same," said John dourly. Samuel Lount and Peter Matthews had been hanged, on April 12, just outside the Toronto jail. Upper Canadians on both sides had begged for Lount's life—his wife on her knees—before the new lieutenant-governor, Sir George Arthur. But he had not revoked his decision to have them hanged as examples. John had heard they were brave to the very end, and even Sheriff Jarvis had shed tears at the gallows when Lount said that God had given him a "great peace in what had happened and in what was going to happen."

"What are you thinking about, John?" Nan asked.

"About Lount and Matthews."

"I thought so. Well, there's no point in doing that now. We can't change what's happened, but we *can* change the future. And look—we're here. I'd better wake the Browns."

The old man made John feed and water the horses while he examined every inch of them. "Youngsters these days—what's their hurry?" he complained. "Travelling that fast, you could have killed my best team." Then Nan went inside and John bedded down in the wagon.

The next morning, the adventurers made their excuses as soon as they could.

"Tell Beatrice I'll have a good visit the day we pick you up to go home," said Great-aunt Eliza. "I'm just not sure when that will be. Could be a week, maybe." An audible groan came from her husband.

Nan smiled sweetly and said, "I'll tell her." Then she and John were off.

"I've got to change my clothes. So I can look like a boy," Nan said.

John stared at her. "Are you serious?" He sighed at the stubborn expression that came over her face, and said resignedly,

182

"Well, you better duck back into the horse stable then."

In a few minutes, they were on their way again. Nan was dressed in her brothers' clothes and had her hair tied up underneath a brown cap with a full top and narrow brim.

"How do I look?" she asked.

"Like a boy—almost," said John, doubtfully.

The youths walked with long strides towards the rebels' meeting place.

17

About thirty men had assembled under the warm May sun. Some of them were sitting in front of the newly planted beds of geraniums and violets on the grey rail fence that surrounded Casey's yard. One man was holding a dipperful of fresh water from the pail that had just been hauled up from the well. Others stood in line, waiting for their turn.

"John!" George's jaw dropped in amazement when he came out on the porch and saw his brother. Immediately, he hurried over. In a low voice, he told his brother to go back home. "Please, John, this is a job for men. I don't want to have to worry about you."

"Why not? I've worried about you plenty, and it didn't hurt me any," was John's retort, and then he added, "I brought a friend along, anyway. We can look out for each other."

George's eyes narrowed. "What friend? Who else have you dragged along?"

"I didn't have to drag her. She wanted to come."

"S*he!*"

John beckoned, and Nan stepped out from behind the lilac bush just behind John, where she'd been waiting.

Mrs. Casey came out on the porch just then, carrying a large platter of sandwiches. The men hurried up to grab the victuals—even those on the fence jumped off and crowded in behind the others. But George stood paralyzed on the spot, staring at Nan. John stepped around to the back of the line-up. He figured he had better get something to eat while he could.

John grabbed a couple for himself and one for Nan. George could look out for himself. When he brought them back, a young man was telling Nan, "Say, you're even shorter than me," as he clapped her heavily on the back. She flinched a little, John thought, but kept her ground, squared her shoulders, and smirked. John was relieved to see the young fellow hadn't realized she was a girl. When he was gone, George came out of his stupor.

"How does Nan happen to be here?" he growled.

Before John could answer, Nan spoke up. "I can speak for myself, George Meyers," she said, pitching her voice as low as she could.

George motioned her to the drive shed. After a while, John followed. Just outside the shed, John could hear his brother's every word. "Are you out of your mind?" George was saying. "You surely aren't planning to come on the raid. And how did you ever get this far?"

"I couldn't bear to sit around worrying about—about everyone. I thought...I thought I could be useful." Nan's voice was hesitant now.

"It's not a game, Nan. This is serious business. And I...
I can't go on if you don't go back."

"George Meyers, you have no right telling me what to do! I'm not your sister."

"No, you're not my sister." George didn't sound angry now. John stepped silently inside the doorway to the shed. He hesitated when he saw his brother and Nan standing close—very close—facing each other in the shadows of the windowless shed.

"I can't order you, but I can ask you..." George said, so softly John could hardly hear.

"Yes?" Nan's voice was pleasant and inviting.

"...to go home. Until I...until we come back."

"All right, George. I'll wait, but..."

John backed away and stood motionless. In a minute, George came out, striding across the yard without a backward glance, his old cocky self. Then Nan came out, blinking in the sunlight. She walked over to John.

"Can you get my pack, John? I left it by the lilac bush. I'm going to go inside and help Mrs. Casey, and I need some proper clothes." She did not look at all upset that her adventure was coming to an end. In fact, she looked downright happy.

That George! He'd charmed the purpose right out of her! Well, I'm not giving up so easily, John thought. He was going to be a part of this adventure, no matter what his brother tried.

Nancy had gone inside, so John wandered about the yard awhile and gathered what information he could. "We'll join the others in Gananoque," said one man. Gananoque was a village fifteen miles east of the town of Kingston. John wondered how they were going to get to Wellesley Island; it was on the U.S. side of the Thousand Islands. Then he heard the name Pirate Bill. Everyone knew Pirate Bill; he and his men made a profession of raiding ships around the Thousand Islands across from Kingston. One or another of them was wanted frequently by both Canadian and American officials. Apparently, this notorious character had been hired to ferry the main force, while smaller boats would carry the others.

"How many do you expect?" someone asked.

"Not many more than this," the first man answered. "Too many will rouse suspicion. It won't take a big gang to do this job—that is, if we take them by surprise."

John thought the crowd in Casey's yard was plenty big already. He wondered what the people living on Wellesley Island would think when they all gathered on its north shore, as they were supposed to do. But then he heard someone say that the island had no permanent settlers.

John needed no further directions. He'd find the Original Road and follow it straight down to where it passed near Adolphustown. Then he'd go east, through Bath and on until he arrived at the turn-off to Kingston. That was the shortest way.

He'd get to the launching spot across from Wellesley Island in time, even if he had to walk all the way—though he might get a ride in a friendly farmer's cart. It was less than thirty miles, and he had until the next night to make it. He could make four miles an hour, almost twice as fast as horses with a heavy load, so that would only take him till nightfall. He'd even have time to stop and sleep at an inn along the way. On second thought, he decided to sleep in a farmer's barn. A hayloft would do just fine.

He went to collect his pack from beneath the lilac bush. He looked back just before he climbed up on the rail fence, to see Nan come out on the porch, now dressed in a light blue overblouse and a royal blue petticoat. She was laughing with Mrs. Casey, and for some reason, John's eyes filled suddenly with hot tears.

Angrily, he brushed them away. Then he hopped the fence and took off.

***

"Who goes there?"

"Meyers, John."

"Who?"

"*Meyers!*" John whispered in the darkening twilight. The sentry at the Gananoque dock wouldn't let him pass. Five other raiders also were milling about, getting ready to jump into the rowboat tied to the dock. The cold, dark waters of the St. Lawrence River slapped and slurped under the wharf, and the small wooden craft bobbed up and down in the choppy waters. The shadowy form of Gladstone Island could barely be discerned, far out in the middle of the river. To the left, a few silhouettes of pines and oak could be made out in the gathering gloom—John's first glimpse of Wellesley Island, the scene of the crime-to-be.

John knew he wasn't going to be a part of this adventure if this thick-headed official didn't let him get to the boat on time. He could tell the man he was George Meyers' brother, but maybe George had told them not to let him join the party.

"I'm *Meyers,*" John repeated rather uselessly, stamping down his foot on the dirt path that led from the dock. "*John Mey—*"

"Hey, John," someone whispered behind him. "Didn't know you were going to be here!" John swivelled around and made out the face of Hugh White, who lived on a farm only a few miles from their own in Sydney Township.

"Here's a fellow who knows me," John said to the apparently deaf guard. "Hugh, tell this fellow who I am."

"George Meyers' brother John," Hugh said immediately. "You know...George Meyers? One of our leaders?"

John rolled his eyes at that, but the sentry looked impressed and let both boys pass on and into the boat with four others.

They started off at once. In the moonlight, John could clearly see another small boatful of rebels filling up and starting to row through the waters. He knew they were also making their way stealthily to Wellesley Island.

A man with a blackened face jabbed John in the ribs. "Here, help yourself," he said, handing him a bucket of soot. "You need to disguise yourself."

John took the bucket, gingerly smeared a few smudges on his cheeks, and passed the container back to the fellow.

"That's not much of a disguise!" said the black-faced man, digging into the bucket and slapping handfuls of soot on John's cheeks and forehead. The horrible stuff drifted into his eyes and made John squint. He couldn't see what difference a "disguise" meant. If they were caught, they'd be identified. And if they got away scot-free, who was to know?

They came ashore then, and John jumped out first. The rest came on his heels, and soon the other small boat too had landed. The water gurgled and churned around the gunwales as six more men tumbled out onto the shore. A man in a blue-check-ered shirt led this crew up to join them.

"Now, men," he said, "I'll lead the way. But in case you lose me, I want you to know where you're going. So listen carefully."

"We're listenin'. Just get on with it!" said a man with a blond beard streaked with black soot. His teeth seemed to be chatter-ing a little.

"We'll go straight south to halfway across this island. It's only a few miles through this bush. Then you'll see water again, to your left. That's the Lake of Isles that runs between Hills Island on the Canadian side and this island on the American side. Just follow that shoreline east to our meeting place behind the refuelling station. You can't miss it—it's the only building on the island, about a hundred feet from shore and right beside it there's a huge pile of wood. We'll board the *Sir Robert Peel* around midnight."

"Let's move out!" said another. The men started to push for-ward just as the other small boat was docking.

"Wait!" said the man. "If we get there ahead of Pirate Bill and the main crew, just stay back in the bush and be quiet. We don't want them to hear us coming. This is important: no talk-ing. Don't go too close."

John had been listening with only one ear while he looked around and wondered where his brothers were. Now he thought that George, at least, was probably a part of that "main crew." He was disappointed. When he had pictured himself here, John had thought his brothers would be around him. They'd be impressed with how stealthy he was, how unafraid. And when it was all over, they'd clap him on the back, and maybe stand him to a drink at the nearest tavern. He hadn't imagined he'd be among strangers, with a dry mouth and a blackened face.

He shivered. So it wasn't going as he had planned. He wouldn't think about that. Nor would he think about Nan, for it brought back that queer ache his heart. No, he'd think about…about politics and rebellion, and the exciting adventures it had brought him so far. Tonight, they would really be striking a blow for reform! There was plenty to think about right here.

It had been a bright night so far. But as the men pushed their way into the woods, a cloud suddenly fell across the moon.

18

"Whoo! Whoo!" An owl hooted from its night-hunting perch somewhere among the pine trees and the fresh-leafed maples. John's body tensed as the posse of raiders ran deeper and deeper into the woods. Barbed raspberry canes whipped against him and cut through his shirt and overalls. He slapped at a few mosquitoes that attacked his face through the horrible soot smell of his camouflage, which should have kept them away. He stumbled over roots and stones as he pushed on, keeping his eyes on the back of the buckskin-coated man ahead. Because the forest was so dense here, that was all he could see of the group.

Moles rustled under the dead leaves on the forest floor, and John thought he heard a heavier tread and a crashing sound. A bear? Not a mother bear, he hoped. More guns were coming with Pirate Bill's crew and would be delivered at their meeting place. But just now, many of the men were empty-handed.

John noticed that the distance between himself and the

buckskin just ahead of him was growing smaller. The man had stopped. When John caught up, he saw they were alone.

"I seem to have lost track of the others," the man mumbled, swatting at mosquitoes in his hair.

"When did you lose sight of them?"

The man couldn't remember.

"Well, can't we just follow the moon? If we keep it in the same position, eventually we'll reach a shore. Then we can follow the shoreline."

"That sounds fine." The man shrugged, content for John to take the lead.

What a dolt, thought John. He had no idea how far astray they'd gone. If *John* had been in the lead, they'd have been there by now!

After a time, he thought he heard water lapping against a shoreline. Once they reached their destination—*if* they did—they would not be far from the United States mainland. He guessed he'd go over with the rest, just to see little Mac, who was still taking refuge there. Would he remember the boy who'd tried to save him from the soupets? The boy who had helped during that fateful week of the Toronto uprising? So much had happened since then…and now he was sixteen, hardly a boy any longer. Still, John thought little Mac would recognize him—if only for his red hair!

John turned left and followed the shore for what seemed like a few miles. Had they ended up at the St. Lawrence River instead of the Lake of Isles? Then, under the glistening moonlight, the steamer itself rose in silhouette against the sky. It was bigger than any ship John had ever seen. And about three hundred yards away, there was the huge wood pile and the supply-keeper's white frame shanty.

John motioned to the man behind him to stop. An owl hooted three times, then three times again. John cupped his hands around his mouth and repeated the sound. The answer came back a little to their right.

Then, light footsteps broke the stillness and about twenty-five men emerged from the bushes and surrounded them.

John was a little alarmed, for these men were armed. Some carried guns and staves. Others had pistols and even swords. Another man looked particularly frightful with a long, red-painted pole that had been whittled into a spear at the end. John's fears were stilled, though, when he saw that his companion had already recognized the men. They were raiders, too, with painted faces.

A hand clapped on John's back. It was George. Bleecker stood right behind him. He'd painted great, long streaks across both his cheeks. He looked ridiculous.

"You're a speedy one, friend. You're the first one here," whispered George. He peered closer. "John, is that you?"

John nodded.

"Well, if that doesn't beat all. Bleecker, it's our *little brother!*"

John was glad the darkness and the soot hid his face from full view. If he looked at George for another second, his head would explode. And Bleecker was gazing down at his youngest brother, shaking his head and "tsking" like an old man. What did *he* know about battles? Not nearly as much as his youngest brother! John felt as if he'd swallowed a large rock of anger and it was lying in the pit of his stomach. Fortunately, he was spared any further conversation.

"Well, men, the time has come," said a big, rugged man with thick, black side burns and hair that curled up at the back of his neck. He wore no trace of the black soot or paint. John suspect-ed this was the Pirate Bill, the scourge of the St. Lawrence. Behind him stood two sturdy fellows who looked so like Bill that John knew they must be his sons.

The rebels crowded together to catch what the burly outlaw was saying. "Thirteen of us will go aboard," he said his eyes flashing in the light of the moon. "We'll send the passengers off the ship. The rest of you including my sons here will stand guard on the shore. Do not, in any circumstances, let the crew mem-bers or passengers get back on the steamer."

"But we're not all here yet," said one of the men from the

back row.

"Well, that's just too bad," said the pirate. "If you wanna wait for them, go right ahead. The rest of us are gettin' on with the night's work. The ship docked at midnight and it's almost two o'clock. She'll not be loitering in this harbour much longer. And the crew ain't gonna wait for us…'cause we ain't got no passenger tickets!" John knew the men wanted to cheer but he could hear only a few chuckles in the semi-darkness.

"Yes, men," said George, acting like the supreme commander, "it's best we move without waiting. I'm volunteering to go aboard. Now, remember, we do not shoot or injure anyone. No rough treatment of passengers, either. These weapons are only for show!"

"Another Lount!" thought John, and a kind of panic seized him. Would George end up on the Toronto gallows, just like the peaceable Quaker?

The men were nodding at George. "You lead us on," said a man John could not see. To John's surprise, Pirate Bill stepped back and shrugged his shoulders, gesturing for George to go ahead of him.

"No," said George, stepping up to stand in front of the men. "I'll not lead, but I'll be right beside you, Bill." He clapped a hand on the pirate's solid shoulder.

"And I'll be right behind George," said Bleecker.

Part of John wanted to leap up then and join his brothers in the vanguard. He opened his mouth to say the words, then clamped it shut again. Something about seeing his brothers with Pirate Bill made him feel like someone's fool little brother, a boy in a man's game.

Still, a strangled squawk escaped. The three men turned slowly and stared in his direction, and John blushed under his disguise. He slunk back into the crowd, hoping no one else had heard him.

"After we get rid of the passengers," Pirate Bill resumed, as if nothing had happened, "the rest of you men can come aboard. Those who wish to go back will be let off farther upstream and the rest will have the honour of sailing with us to the United States."

There was a muted cheer, and Pirate Bill, George, and Bleecker crept out silently with nine chosen men. Each was armed with a pistol. First, they headed back into the cover of the trees. The rest of the men followed, holding back the branches for each other in order to move more silently through the underbrush. When they reached the spot directly opposite the wharf, they crouched and waited. The keeper's shanty near the woodpile was still in darkness.

Soon, ten of the ship's crew members came marching along the wharf and the shoreline and headed straight for the woodpile. They stacked big piles of wood in their arms, their backs turned from the shore, their steamship, and the hidden rebels. Twelve dark forms emerged from the bush, making a run for the docking area. They crossed the wharf and hit the wooden gang-plank, still in silence. Then the second team of raiders strode over to the edge of the wharf to block the sailors from boarding their ship again.

John took a position on the ground just to the left of the wharf. He shivered a little. Even though the night was warm, it was still very dark. Suddenly, he wished he wasn't there at all. He could easily end up hanging from the gallows—and so could George and Bleecker. And even if they did escape to the States, what would be the point of that? Upper Canada was his home. Exile seemed a poor, second-choice kind of life.

But now a couple of the sailors had noticed the raiders at their backs with pistols pointed. They stiffened and gasped. In an instant, the entire crew had dropped their loads on the ground and raised their arms. "Don't touch your guns," shouted more than one raider. Looking more closely, John could see that only one of the sailors had a gun.

Half the raiders held back the crew, while the others turned to watch the ship. There was a tramping of feet and the passen-gers started coming out. John saw immediately that George was no Lount—the women and girls had not been spared a moment to dress, or even to pack a bag. They were wearing only cotton nightgowns and shawls. Though he felt sorry for them, John couldn't help smiling at the younger women with white flannel knots sticking out all over their heads—curling rags. Their faces were streaked with tears and smudges. They looked worse than the raiders.

Older men in long nightshirts with fat stomachs and skinny legs looked just as ridiculous as they padded across the wharf behind the women. A number of bald men missing their wigs glared in silence as they stepped onto the green grass.

"You'll be sorry!" screamed an old lady, who stopped in front of one of the Belleville boys and poked her cane straight at his stomach. She moved on to the next one and thwacked him on the head.

"Watch out, old crone," snarled the man, rubbing his injury. "You might get that cane wrapped around your neck!"

"Hmmph," she said, tapping her cane loudly on the wooden wharf as she stomped along beyond the men. The raiders standing on either side of John started a low chant: "Revenge for the *Caroline!*" they kept repeating. "Revenge for the *Caroline!*" The chorus echoed in John's ears.

The passengers headed for the keeper's shanty. The first women there pounded on the door with their fists and arms, screaming loudly, "Help! Help! Open up!"

Candlelight flickered in the window next to the door. John breathed more easily now that the women had found shelter.

Then a latecomer from the ship, a grey-haired woman wrapped in an elegant, blue satin dressing gown, stepped serenely along the wooden planks of the wharf. Her hair was all askew, but apart from that, she did not look helpless at all. She had managed to pack a carpetbag full of her belongings; perhaps that was why she was the last to leave the steamer. She glared straight at John as if he were a schoolboy caught eating cookies in class, then swept the other men in one blazing glance. "You'll pay for this," she said to them.

"Oh, yeah?" shouted one raider as he grabbed her bag and wrenched it from her hand. She reached up to swat him across the face, but he caught her hand and bent it backwards.

The woman cried out in pain.

John jumped forward. "You heard George!" he shouted at the man. "No one is to be hurt! This is no battle against women! Give me the bag!"

The man grumpily handed the case to John, who held it out to the woman.

She whipped the bag from John's hand and said, "Thank you. I'm glad to see there are a few moral men left, even among thieves." With her head held high and her back straight and stiff, she walked sedately on to join the others.

201

Thieves! The word echoed in John's ears. He had never been called a thief before. Were they really thieves? No. This was war, and seizing the ship was part of their strategy. Why, these very women would be hailing them as heroes, once the Reformers and their democratic southern neighbours freed them all from tyranny.

Still, John thought he'd feel better about the whole thing if they just got going. The passengers and crew were all off the ship—why weren't George and the others giving them a signal to board? The moon disappeared behind dark clouds, and the darkness seemed to engulf the raiders and their victims. A frightening silence closed in.

"There must be trouble," mumbled the man who'd first handed John the pail of soot.

"Someone'd better go and check," said another.

"I'll go," said John. Before anyone could protest, John shot ahead, running across the wharf, and then along the gangplank.

Jumping onto the ship's deck, he stood and listened for a few seconds, wondering which way to go. He heard voices but could not make out any words.

Then loud shouting erupted. "Revenge for the *Caroline!*" The raiders who'd boarded the ship came running past, jumped onto the gangplank, and piled onto the wharf, still shouting in unison, "Revenge for the *Caroline!*"

Turning, John saw flames leaping into the darkness at the far end of the ship. More men raced by. Where were George and Bleecker?

Then he felt himself being pulled up by the arm and turned about. He looked up into George's face.

"C'mon. The ship's afire!"

"But I thought—"

"We couldn't get her going. Not even Pirate Bill knew how to run her—she has new-fangled parts and we couldn't figure it out. She's been set on fire and cut adrift. Hurry!"

John leapt onto the gangplank right after George, and they both hit the wharf running.

As his feet touched the grass on the shore, Bleecker fell into step on the other side of John. The three Meyers boys charged ahead and into the woods. They were at the tail end of the rebel band.

John figured he'd stay between George and Bleecker. That way he would not get lost. Besides, they had guns tucked in their belts.

***

Streaks of pale light appeared in the eastern sky as Pirate Bill's boat approached the long dock at Kingston Harbour. A handful of enterprising seagulls flew overhead, and a few stray cats roamed along the shoreline, sniffing for fish. But otherwise, the harbour was deserted.

They had come close to being sighted. About five miles from Wellesley Island, the *Oneida*, a local steamship, had gone by, heading southeast. John was glad, for it meant the burning ship would be spotted and its passengers rescued soon. But George and Bleecker hadn't been so happy. "They'll have the whole military waiting for us on the mainland," said Bleecker. "Bad news travels fast." So Pirate Bill had brought them to Kingston rather than back to Gananoque.

John was the first to jump up on the dock. George and Bleecker were close on his heels, and about twenty-five ragged raiders followed. They all stood together on the dock, watching Pirate Bill Johnston, his remaining crew, and his two stalwart sons turn the boat around.

"Thanks, Sir William!" shouted one of the raiders, and they all saluted, grinning. The reference was to the British Colonel MacNab, who had been knighted after he'd destroyed the American ship *Caroline*. The new "Sir William" returned their salute, then set sail for his stronghold on Abel's Island, on the U.S. side of the river.

"Crowds attract attention," said George. "We must separate...and Godspeed." The raiders nodded in agreement, and all moved off in different directions. George, Bleecker, and John stayed together and began racing west along the shore of Lake Ontario.

19

A crow flew over the freshly seeded fields of corn on a farm a few miles south of Napanee. He was hoping to make a meal of the kernels under the young, green shoots. As he was busy ripping up a half-dozen plants at the end of the row, three figures emerged from the woods and skulked along the edge of the field in the light of the rising sun. It was the thirty-first of May, 1838, and the three Meyers brothers had been travelling since the previous morning, stopping only for brief intervals and a few hours' sleep the night before. George and Beecker had stubbly beards, and John had telltale bits of soot stuck in his red hair.

At mid-morning, they stopped and sprawled out under a clump of ash trees to munch on the last bits of dried fruit in John's knapsack. By noon, they'd reached Napanee and headed straight for Casey's house. The place looked the same as usual with the rail fence, the newly planted geranium flowerbeds, and the big maple tree in the backyard.

"I'll go in and ask for Nan," said John, looking sideways at George.

"That's a good idea," he answered. "We'll stay in the shade of the maple tree till you tell us the coast is clear. They won't suspect you of anything. Anyway, the news may not have reached them yet."

John stepped up to the front door and knocked as his brothers slinked around to the back of the house.

John knocked, the door swung open, and he was staring into the surprised eyes of the stout but dignified Mrs. Casey. "Come in!" she burst out. She grabbed him by the arm and almost closed the door on his knapsack as she pulled him inside. "We've been worrying about you boys. The Belleville militia met the messenger from the Kingston militia on the road coming here. They're scouting around for all strays like you!"

"Oh, John, I'm so glad you're all right!" Nan flew around the corner of the hall doorway and flung her arms around John. His heart lifted with hope, and he hugged Nan back, forgetting all about his brothers. In a moment, though, Nan pushed him away and stepped back, her nose wrinkling.

Then George strode in, with Bleecker right behind. Nan rushed to the second Meyers, then stopped short.

"Why, George Meyers, you smell, too!"

John inwardly rejoiced at George's sour expression. His

handsome brother was not used to this kind of welcome.

Before Nan had a chance to say another word, she was interrupted by a loud banging at the front door. Mrs. Casey ran to her parlour, pulled back her heavy green velvet curtains, and gasped. She turned and scurried back to the kitchen. "It's the sheriff. Quick! Hide in the attic over the shed. He may want to search the place. There've been rumours."

Nan led the boys out into the shed. They could hear more loud banging as they scuffled up the ladder to the attic. "I'm coming, I'm coming," said Mrs. Casey, pretending to sound impatient. She flicked up some flour off the kitchen table as she passed.

"You'd think there was a fire," she said as loudly as she could without actually shouting. She clapped her hands together and the flour made a white cloud between them as she opened the door. "My bread will drop now for sure. There's a special knack to good bread, you know.... Well, if it isn't Sheriff Ruttan. Now, what can I do for you?"

"You can get me that husband of yours. We hear he's been up to no good."

"Well, he's at work. Didn't you stop by his blacksmith's shop?"

"No, we figured we'd catch him at home during the noon hour."

"Maybe he's on his way. But I packed him bread and cheese this morning. Sometimes he doesn't make it home at noon."

"What if we ask to search the place?"

"Fine with me. But you'll do it over my dead body unless you take off those boots."

"Oh, very well, I'll look in at the shop first."

"What seems to be the trouble?" Mrs. Casey asked in a more congenial tone.

"The militia from Belleville are down here, trying to round up some men who've been up to no good. They've even brought back the old militia fellows, with Captain Meyers leading the troops."

Captain Meyers? In the dim light of the shed attic, his fugitive sons exchanged looks.

"Is that so? Well, I think you'll find my husband occupied in his shop. I doubt he knows a thing. He's been hard at it with all the spring work."

"Thank you, ma'am."

Mrs. Casey waited about fifteen minutes. Then she called for Nan. "Watch by the window," Mrs. Casey said as Nan entered the parlour, "but stand back and do not draw the curtain. Tell me at once if you see anyone approach our gate."

Mrs. Casey bustled out of the room, through the kitchen, and up the ladder to the little attic over the shed. "Come down, quickly," she said, sliding back the wooden slab that acted as a door. The brothers almost fell out.

"Did you hear?" she asked. They all nodded.

"Where can we go?" George asked, raking his now matted brown hair with his fingers.

"I don't know, but maybe you could head north. The way from Belleville to Kingston is well patrolled. You could try going south to Hay Bay, but it's probably patrolled by boats. I just don't know."

"We'll go north," said Bleecker. "But it's hard to travel in broad daylight."

Nan called from the window, where she still was on the lookout. "I'll go with you. It'll throw them off their guard."

"She's right," said Mrs. Casey. "Now give me your empty sacks. There's water in the basin, and here's coal oil and washrags. You may think you did a good job getting off that soot and war paint in some pond on the road, but you didn't. Now get to work!"

While the boys washed, Mrs. Casey and Nan threw victuals into their packs: bread, huge chunks of cheese, dried apple chunks, hickory nuts, and a flask of water.

Nan ran upstairs to get her pack while Mrs. Casey plopped a big jar of bear grease into John's bag . That would keep off the black flies and mosquitoes—though John thought it might be a bit too late. He didn't think there was an inch of bare skin on him that didn't already have a bite .

"We'll have to split up now," said George, and John's hopes died. He had an idea of who would go with whom. But George surprised him. "John, you and Nan go first. The two of you will be safer without us."

"We can go north at first," John suggested, "and when we get far enough, we'll double back south and head home."

"Good idea," said George. "Nan needs to get home to her parents. They'll be worried. Start off there as soon as you can."

"Wait a minute," said Bleecker. "There's a commotion in the backyard."

Someone pounded on the front door.

"The house is surrounded!" It was the sheriff's voice.

"Hide in the shed," said George, turning to Nan and John.

Bleecker nodded. "We'll distract them out front. Get out as soon as you can. Walk until you reach the edge of town. Then— run!"

John and Nan waited inside the back shed, breathing fast and shallow. Bleecker went to the front, with George right behind, and opened the door.

There was a silent pause, then—

"Hello, Father. What are *you* doing in Napanee?" asked Bleecker.

20

Father!

A hundred thoughts whirled in John's head as he and Nan hurried through town. Would George be able to think up a story right there on the doorstep that could convince the sheriff that all was in order? Would Father play along? And if it didn't work...John was sure Father wouldn't want to take his own sons into custody, but if he didn't, he would risk arrest himself.

And what about Bleecker? John had no worries about George—he had proved himself in Toronto, half a year ago. But Bleecker was more cautious, more used to playing by the rules. What if they threatened to harm his family if he didn't confess? Bleecker had been a ringleader in this whole affair; no one would be safe if he talked—not Pirate Bill, not any of the Belleville men, and not John.

John looked fearfully over his shoulder.

"Stop doing that!" hissed Nan. "It makes you look like a fugitive!"

They hurried north along Centre Street. As they approached Macpherson's Mill, John shifted his pack and Nan tucked her hair under her cap. As soon as they were past the old stone building, they broke into a run. The landscape became a blur of brown, blue, and green as they pelted along the corduroy road that led north out of Napanee.

After ten minutes, Nan slowed down.

"I can't…keep…this…up," she gasped.

"You have to. We've got to get as far north as we can."

Nan's breathing slowed. "I don't understand why, exactly," she said.

John patiently explained. "The militia is bound to check all the regular routes to and from Napanee—probably they'll even have a patrol on the Appenea River. But they're not so likely to take the northern route. It's full of marshes and streams, and the road becomes nothing but a twisting trail."

"Well, what if we get lost? I'd rather get caught…at least there's the chance of talking your way out. Why, I bet George is spinning a yarn to that sheriff right this minute." She smiled, smoothed her coat, and tucked her hair back under her cap. "I wonder what he's saying?"

"We won't get lost. I still have my compass," said John

shortly; then, because he'd been thinking about it, he added, "I bet George says he was helping out in Casey's Blacksmith Shop and intends to sign on as apprentice."

"That's a likely story, but would your father go along? George would be asking his father to lie for him."

John shrugged. "George is thinking seriously about becoming a saddler. He's always liked handling horses and has made some fine saddles and harness." John was about to describe one of the saddles George had made, but Nan was starting to look a bit too interested in hearing about his older brother's talents. So he stopped before he started. He and Nan were going to be together for a while and he intended to make the best of it.

The two resumed walking.

"What will happen if someone from the steamship recognized your brothers?" asked Nan.

"I doubt anyone would have. None of us looked much like ourselves with all that paint and soot on our faces. But if…if they *are* identified, they'll be held till the July assizes. Then they'll be tried for treason."

"They'll be… You mean they could be…hanged?"

"Don't think the worst!" John said this more crossly than he'd meant to, simply becuase he was anxious himself. He softened his tone. "Father will think of some way to help. After all, George got off his Toronto escapade without any trial. Father has lots of friends."

"George was so brave," said Nan. "He went through all that time in a Toronto jail, but it didn't stop him. He went right into it again—to help the cause!"

"And just what is the cause?" asked John.

"John! How can you ask such a thing?" Nan stopped walking until he turned squarely around and looked at her.

"I don't know.… I guess I'm beginning to have some questions about it all. I wonder what we really accomplished with this raid." John was staring down at the dusty road now, wondering why he'd ever felt excited about fighting. "It seems pretty hopeless. Just a bunch of disorganized hooligans."

"I've never heard you talk like this before, John. What's happened to change your views?"

"Nothing, really. I still feel that democracy will come sooner or later. I just want it to come peacefully. I don't want us to go through what the Americans did. I don't want a revolution."

Nan was silent, digesting this. Without looking at her, John added, "It was frightening, but more than that, the raid was…demeaning. That's what bothered me the most. One lady referred to us as a bunch of 'thieves.'"

"Why did she say that?"

"I guess she thought we were going to take her belongings. I returned her bag. One of the raiders had grabbed it, but he didn't want it! He was just being mean. War and battles bring out the cruelty in people. It bothers me."

Nan frowned. "I know that Christ said we were to 'turn the other cheek.' But does that mean we're supposed to tolerate oppression? Doesn't the Bible also say something about putting on the armour of God to fight for truth and justice?"

John sighed. "I don't know. Lount tried to do it the peaceful way, and look where it got him! Myself, I've always found it very hard not to fight back!"

Nan grinned. "I've heard it's especially hard for people with red hair!"

"What?!" John spluttered. "It has nothing to do with my hair!" What a thing to say. Nan had completely wrecked the mood.

For a while, only the crunching of their feet could be heard along the road. Then Nan reached up and ruffled John's curls.

"Don't be angry, John," she said. "I've always liked your red hair. That's why I tease you so much about it."

"Honest?" said John, and Nan nodded solemnly. "Maybe it's not so bad," conceded John. "At least it's distinctive!" He laughed. "Still, do you know what I can't figure out? Why William Lyon Mackenzie wore a red wig! Why would anyone choose red if they had all the colours to pick from?"

"I guess it was the colour of his real hair." Nan smiled. "Or perhaps his wife likes red hair, the same as I do."

John smiled back at Nan. He linked his arm with hers and they walked on in silence.

After a time, they became aware of the clip-clop of horses' hooves behind them. Nan turned first. "Look!" She pointed to a team of bay horses speeding along the road and gaining fast. "We'd better dive into the bushes."

John shook his head. "He's already seen us, Nan. We'll only look suspicious if we head for the fields."

"What if he stops us?" Nan was starting to look nervous.

"I'll handle it. Don't say a word—just wave and smile as he goes by. That way we'll look innocent. Now, let me think."

They had walked only a hundred yards more when they heard the team slowing down beside them. The wagon contained what looked like bags of ground grain. The driver must be returning from the mill. John and Nan were so relieved it was not the sheriff or one of the militia that the happiness in their smiles and greetings was genuine.

"Where are you folks headed?" the farmer asked.

John was ready. "Up north, beyond Kaladar. Father wanted us to visit his mother. And Mother has sent a few things for Grandma." He pointed to their bags.

"She's not been too well lately," added Nan. John shot her a glance in warning. She musn't put in too much.

"Well, jump on. As it happens, I'm going that way, too. I've just been down to Napanee to have my grain ground. I had to get supplies, too."

"We'd be mighty obliged to you, sir. My sister's getting kind of tired," John said, grabbing the side of the wagon and pulling himself up. Then he gave Nan his hand to pull her up beside him. The driver didn't look any older than George. And he had light red hair, much the same as John's.

"Say, this seat is kind of crowded," John said. "Do you mind if we sit in the back and give you more room?"

John saw the man hesitate. He guessed he didn't want to turn his back on them. So maybe the fellow was a little suspicious. "That's all right, John," Nan said, trying to smooth over the situation. "I'd sooner sit up here." She smiled up at the man, her dark eyes flashing and friendly.

"Sure, you go ahead, sonny." The farmer was talking to John, but he was smiling down at Nan.

John didn't feel too easy about the situation, but Nan didn't seem the least bit uncomfortable. In fact, she seemed to be enjoying herself—a little bit too much. She sure was getting to be a flirt. He settled down on the grain bags quietly in order not to miss any of their conversation.

"So, what's *your* name?"

"Nan," she said without hesitation. "What's yours?"

"James."

"Are you from around these parts?" the farmer asked.

"Not really. We're from Belleville. We travelled to Napanee with an elderly couple to help them with the driving. Now, we're going north to visit our grandma."

"What's her name?"

"Well, she's been married five times and outlived all her husbands. I don't rightly know which name she's using now."

"Well, isn't that a fright."

"Yes, she's really a hermit. I hope she recognizes us. Ma was awfully worried about her when she and Pa visited last fall. But she wouldn't come back with them. Says she's gonna stay in her own place till the end."

"She sounds like a holy terror!"

John groaned to himself. The more outragious the story, the harder it would be to keep it up. Nan had better be careful!

"Now, how about you?" she asked. "I suppose you're married with two or three kids by now."

"Can't say that I am. There's no near neigbours, and I'm the last one at home. I never seem to have time to go courting. But one of these days, I will. Ma says she needs more help in the kitchen, and I'd best find me a wife. I plan to go down to Napanee someday and just look around."

"Do you think that's all it will take?"

"Sure! We got a big farm and my pa is known in the town. Many a girl would be glad of such a fine home."

"I suppose," said Nan, rather coldly. John was starting to sweat. If Nan started arguing with the driver, they'd both be out walking again—soon. And now that he was sitting, he began to realize how really tired he was. He'd had little sleep last night and none the night before.

"Now, let me guess," said Nan pleasantly again. "Are you looking for someone with chestnut or raven-black hair?"

John relaxed a little. Perhaps Nan *could* take care of herself. He laid his head on a soft bag of ground grain. The familiar smell was soothing. The voices grew fainter.

***

"John! John!" It was Nan, leaning over the back of the front seat and shaking him by the shoulder.

John could hear the farmer laughing out loud. "He sure was dead to the world." John looked around and saw the sun had begun to set. They had come a long way—maybe past Kaladar.

"Well, I'm turning east here," said James. "Would you like to go on home with me? It's only about five miles east on this road."

"We'd love to…," Nan began.

John rubbed his eyes open, and then everything came back to him. He and Nan should circle back west to Belleville and not east. "No," he said sharply. "We can't be far from Kaladar. We can stay there."

"We're two miles *past* Kaladar," James shot back, "and I'm offering you a meal and a free overnight stop."

Nan looked questioningly at John. "Well?" she asked.

"No, we'd better keep going to Grandma's," he muttered.

"Why do you let your little brother boss you around?" James asked. He gave John a miserable stare.

Nan smiled and said, "Well, just because he's a boy, he thinks he knows better. I'm glad *some* men aren't like that."

James smiled in appreciation and blushed to his roots. "Nan, would you give me your address?" he stammered. "Maybe I could come to see you, sometime—if the folks will let me away long enough."

"I live the other side of Belleville on a farm in Sydney Township. My name's Nan Burditt. You can write to me, but I don't know if you should come to see me. You see, my pa's awful strict."

"So that's why you're running off with this one?"

John almost bit his tongue. Now they were in trouble. After a short silence, Nan asked, "What makes you think we're running off? He's my *brother!*"

"Well…he calls his parents 'Mother' and 'Father,' and you call yours 'Ma' and 'Pa.'"

Nan wasn't the least bit ruffled. "Oh, John's always been different from the rest of us."

"Then why is he so insanely jealous of you? Brothers couldn't care less about their sisters talking to fellows."

John was about to explode. His face had gone even redder than the young man's. "Are you trying to pick a fight?" he yelled at the farmer.

"Don't mind if I do." James started to peel off his jacket.

"Now, John." Nan held him back with a grip like iron, but her voice was smooth. "John is just protective of me. That's the way our parents taught him. When you visit, you'll see." She smiled at him and lowered her eyelashes. "I would like you to visit me…sometime."

Where did she learn all this? John wondered with suspicion. This was not a Nan he'd ever seen. Or perhaps Nan wasn't so completely taken up with George after all. If that was so, there might still be a chance for *him*.

"You come up to Belleville in July after the hay crop is in. You'll have more time then," Nan suggested. She took the man's hand as she jumped down lightly from the wagon seat.

"I'll be seeing you, Nan." He could hardly take his eyes off her.

Nan just smiled and waved again. James jumped back up on his seat, whipped his team into a run, and was away. John could see he was trying to show off.

John walked briskly along for about fifteen minutes without saying a word. Then he said, "There's a clump of trees over there. You can change your clothes there and become a young man again like you were on the way down here."

Nan stopped and planted her hands on her hips. "John Meyers! I'll change only because it's easier to travel that way, now we're in rougher trails with all these swamps." Then she looked sideways at him. "Whatever got into you, John? Anyone would think you were sweet on me, the way you acted, so jealous and everything!"

John stared. Was it possible that she didn't know? And if he made his feelings clearer…

Nan didn't wait for an answer, but plunged between the spruce branches with her bag in hand.

"Why'd you give him your real name and address?" John called out.

"Oh, that," Nan's voice was muffled. "By the time he takes me up on my offer to visit, all the uproar over the boat attack will have died down. Besides…" She emerged from the trees, dressed like a boy again, so the rest of her words had an odd effect. "…he did seem like a nice young man. Maybe Pa's heard of his family."

"So you hope," John said darkly. "It's never wise to trust strangers. Maybe James belongs to a gang of outlaws! He never did give us his last name!"

"Don't be crazy, John!"

John smiled. Maybe he *was* being ridiculous. He gave Nan a soft punch on the arm.

"We'd better get going, 'Ned,'" he said. "See if you can keep up with my manly pace."

They set off briskly in the growing dusk.

21

"If I never see another hill, rock, creek, or lake, it will be too soon!"

Nan was sitting on a big stone in the warm afternoon light, but her mood was far from sunny. "I think we've come far enough. Can we please turn back towards home now? If you know where we are, that is."

It was late on the third day since the pair had left Napanee, and even though the land was sparsely populated, they'd managed to find food and places to sleep: at a farmer's house the first night and at a fisherman's cabin the next. They'd caught a couple of rides since James; there weren't many farmers in the area, but the few who were there had seeded their crops and had a bit of time before hay cutting to make trips to town for supplies. And they were always willing to take on a couple of passengers on the return trip.

When John and Nan didn't have rides, they walked fast, and

even ran sometimes. But they'd covered little ground today. No wagons had passed them on the road, and the trail was rough, zigzagging east and west around scores of streams and bogs. This land was wild and unsettled, full of evergreens and out-crops of speckled granite.

Now they'd entered a more heavily wooded area. They were surrounded by white and red oaks and Jack pines. Huge white pines stretched above the other treetops in many places, waving and sighing as the wind brushed their featherlike needles. It was real forest, and John loved it. If it weren't for Nan and the fact that he had no gun for hunting, he'd want to go on and on. He wondered if Samuel de Champlain and the other explorers had felt the same way. Was that what kept them going, despite the bugs and the weather? This feeling of something wonderful just around the next bend in the trail?

"John? John!" He turned to look at Nan. "You're a million miles away. You didn't hear a word I said."

"I'm sorry," said John. "Tomorrow, we'll turn southwest towards home. Come on, we've rested long enough."

"Not that. I asked you where we are." Nan sighed deeply and got to her feet.

"Well, I think we're—"

"John Meyers! Do you mean to say you've got us *lost?*"

"Well, if the area's not really well known, I can't give it a name, can I?" said John irritably. "But I think we're near the rock shoreline of Mazinaw Lake."

Nan didn't look quite so worried now. "I've heard of that place. They say it sounds wonderful when your voice bounces back from the great big cliff. But I want to head back home, militia or no militia. I'd just as soon meet them as the bears."

So *she'd* been thinking about bears, too. "Don't worry!" he assured her—and himself. "That wind coming from the south will carry our scent right to them. They'll get out of our way fast enough. Bears only attack when they're startled." He didn't mention that mother bears might act differently.

Suddenly, he stopped. "Look, Nan, there are blue streaks through these trees. Just look!"

Nan peered ahead as she moved through the young oak underbrush that John had parted for her. "You're right," she exclaimed. "Do you think it's Lake Mazinaw? Have we reached the big rock?"

"I'm sure of it."

John was right. They had come out on the edge of a lake and were looking across it at a sheer cliff that rose straight up more than three hundred feet from the waterline. The cliff was almost a mile long. John looked down to the deep blue clear water at his own feet. He could see the steep incline for only a few feet out, and then it was lost from sight.

"Nan...Nan," John called out.

"Nan...Nan." The echo came back across the waves.

"John...John," Nan called and her words were also repeated.

Then the two fugitives called out rhymes and songs until they were breathless. Nan was enjoying herself so much that John hated to stop her. When he got tired of it, he sat on a stone and gazed at the girl he loved. Her eyes were bright and snapping, her musical voice echoed back over the waters and into the trees. He'd never forget his adventure, and he'd always remember Nan, just like this—filthy clothes and all.

Then John saw the clouds rolling up over the lake, and he knew he had to break the spell. "Nan," he said gently, "we have some food left in our knapsacks. Do you want something to eat?"

"Oh, yes, yes! I'm starving. I'm sorry...it's been so much fun. How long have we been here?"

"About half an hour, I reckon."

"Half an hour? So long..." Her eyes were dreamy. The wilderness had caught her in its spell as well.

John wrapped his coat around Nan's shoulders. "We better get on our way!"

Nan trudged along while John tried to locate a good spot to build a shelter. It was so damp they could almost feel the rain before it hit.

They had not gone far when the wind and rain came in sheets, whipping their clothes about them and soaking their outer garments. Nan was a little better off, because she was still wearing John's heavy coat. But John's drenched shirt lay tight against his back.

How can I make a shelter now? John wondered. With cold rain pelting down on their heads and streaming from their noses and chins, they ran ahead, searching desperately for any sort of ready-made shelter. Nan clasped John's wet hand in her own, and clung to it.

John stopped abruptly and pulled her close to him under a cottonwood tree. There was a little shelter under the drooping branches. The sky lit up with the flash of lightning, followed instantly by a thundering crash. A tree only a few yards away was split right in two and a heavy branch fell to the one side as sparks ignited the tree.

Nan screamed in terror.

Then, just as suddenly, the tree fire was put out as the rain began teaming down in torrents again.

John said quietly, "I don't think we should stay under this tree. It could be hit, too."

Still hand in hand, they staggered on until they were completely out of breath. They leaned against a huge rock. The rain was just dripping off them. Then John felt the rock give a little under him. He must be imagining things—he'd been blown around so much by the wind and the rain, he was probably a bit feverish. But the rock moved again. This time he was sure of it!

"Nan?" John whispered.

"Yes, John."

"Can you step away from the rock for a minute?" She looked up at him as if he was crazy but moved over anyway. John struggled to push the big stone aside. It seemed to move a little more. Then, after he gave the stone a mighty push, it gave way and rolled a foot or so. Behind it was a black hole—an opening about two feet wide.

"Look!" said John. "Let's go in. We'll be out of the rain!"

"Have you gone mad?" said Nan. "There could be a bear in there."

"I'm willing to risk it," said John grimly. "You can stay out here and get wetter, if you want."

"Well, you look around first," said Nan. In spite of John's coat, Nan was shivering so much that her teeth were actually chattering.

John squeezed through the opening and stumbled around a little in the pitch dark. The place was dry and smelled only of old moss and leaves, not bears. "C'mon, Nan," he yelled. "It's all right."

Without further hesitation, she stooped and crawled into

the cave, bumping against John, who was standing only a few feet inside.

"Oh, John," she moaned. "This wasn't a good idea, at all. I'm tired of adventures. I just want to go home!" She was sobbing. He put his arm around her shoulders, and after a while, she stopped crying. "Thank you, John. I'm sorry I broke down," she sniffed. "I'm usually braver than this, aren't I?"

"Don't worry about it," said John. He felt warmer now, out of the wind. It didn't seem so dark anymore, either. There was light, coming from…somewhere. Maybe there was a hole in the top of the cave, farther inside. Well, now wasn't the time to explore. He'd do that tomorrow.

Out of the wind and rain, they sat still for a time and listened to the storm, which was still so close it was frightening.

"How silly—we both have dry clothes in our bags," Nan said. "I could change back into my blouse and petticoat." She was right. They were a little damp, but the leather of the bags had kept off the worst of the rain.

"There's not much room to change," he said.

"We'll manage," she replied. "You turn around."

John managed to change into his fresh overalls and shirt without banging into the sides of the cave or Nan. But they sure were in close quarters.

"We can share your coat, John," Nan said, wrapping his coat

around them both and then, with their backs towards the wall, they huddled there together, their hands clasped. Nan was still shivering, so John put an arm around her again, and soon warmed up. After all, it was almost summer.

***

John woke to the stillness of early morning. He was still sitting against the wall, but Nan had fallen across his lap in her sleep. He stroked her long hair and wanted to stay there forever.

He had not been sitting there long before Nan woke suddenly and looked up into his eyes. "John, I was dreaming we were in a cave."

"We are," John laughed. Streaks of light were just beginning to shine into the entrance, only about five feet away.

They both stared outside and watched in silence as rays of the early morning sun streamed inside.

"I think we should get going," said Nan.

"You're right," said John, "but I'd like to look around a bit." John leaned against the wall and stood up. He could actually stand up straight. Not bad for a cave. Then he turned towards the back of the cave and shouted.

"Look, Nan!" He pointed up.

Nan turned and looked up at the roof of the cave. Dripping from the ceiling were what appeared to be shiny icicles.

"Those can't be icicles," John said. "The shine must be coming from somewhere else…" He looked around, and could not believe his eyes. Was it really what he thought?

Nan gasped. "It's the *Silver Cave!*"

It was true. Streaks and flakes of silver in the rock caught whatever light there was and illuminated the whole area around them, even where they'd slept. John took a few steps farther into the cave. The stalactites were even larger there, hanging from the roof like big silver icicles, reflecting the shining flakes of silver across the walls.

John started running deeper into the cave, his red hair even more brilliant in the silvery light.

"Come back here, John Meyers!" Nan shouted. "Come back! Come back!"

But with great energy, John kept going farther, mesmerized by the shining silver flakes on the rock walls. Nan was screaming, "You'll get lost in there. You'll *die* for that silver—just like your ancestors!"

He grinned. He wasn't going to die! He was going to live, live, live! He'd buy that big farm he'd always wanted. And he'd marry Nan. And they'd have one hundred cows and five hired men and he'd give her the biggest house in Sydney Township—maybe in the whole Midland District.

The veins of silver were growing wider now. John was about

to go around another corner when he realized he could no longer hear Nan's voice.

"Nan! Where are you?" There was no answer but his own panting breath. He tried to breathe more quietly, and listened closely. Finally, he heard a banging sound. She must be signalling him by beating stones against the wall of the cave. He followed the sound.

"John! John! John!" Finally, he heard her screaming voice.

"John!" she gasped when he came into sight at last. "Sometimes I think *all* you Meyerses are crazy!" John could see tears in her eyes.

"I'm sorry," John said, pulling Nan towards him and wiping her tears with his shirt sleeve. "I guess I *have* gone a bit crazy. All my life, I've heard tales about this cave. All my life, I've wanted to find it. And we...we stumbled right into it!"

"Yes, but now that you've seen it, what're you going to do about it? We can't dig up the cave and take it home with us!"

John wasn't listening. He seized Nan's hand in his. "Nan, I haven't spoken before this, because I had nothing to offer you. But now I do. I love you, Nan Burditt. All this will be yours if you only say the word!"

"Oh, John..." Tears had made tracks in the dirt on her cheeks; her hair had come loose from her cap and was tangled and filled with pine needles and leaf fragments. But she had never looked more beautiful to John. She gazed around at the gleaming silver that surrounded them. Her glance returned to John's expectant face, and she lowered her eyes and looked at the ground.

"I…I just want to…to go home," Nan said.

She hadn't given him an answer. She hadn't said yes—but she hadn't said no, either. John dropped her hand.

"Let's get to work. I don't know that I'll ever find this cave again, so we must take as much as we can carry. Don't worry—you'll get your share."

John wedged his way out of the cave and picked up a big stone. Then he came back inside, snapped his knife out of his belt, and dug into a vein of silver. He pounded the end of his knife with the stone. The silver gave way easily. "Silver is softer and much lighter than stone," he said. He picked it up and handed it to Nan. "Here—that's my gift for you, Nan…my first gift."

She smiled, a bit doubtfully. "I'd rather have something to eat, right now," she said. But she took the silver from his hand and slipped it into one of the pockets under her petticoat.

"I'll go fishing first. Then we'll have lots of energy for digging," he said. "I'll bet there are lots of big fish in the lake."

Nan sighed and sat on a stone. "I may hate the sight of this cave before we leave this place. Remember, you promised to start home today, John Meyers!"

John wasn't listening. He was already heading for Lake Mazinaw, whittling the end of a strong branch to make a fishing spear. Now that it was daylight, he could see streaks of the clear blue waters shining through the trees. It was going to be a fine day.

22

"Well, the two of you are a sight for sore eyes!" Jane gasped as he and Nan came bursting into her kitchen in Belleville.

Nan was still wearing her brother's trousers, but there was a large rip in the left knee and the right cuff had disappeared altogether. Her face was smeared with mud, and she'd flung her petticoat across her shoulder. John was hunched under the weight of two knapsacks, one hanging in front and one on his back. His light cap was pulled down low over his brow. His hair was straggling down his neck and the light red stubble on his face had turned into something resembling a beard. It had been a hard journey. They'd been lost more than once, but John had always been able to keep them going in the right direction with his compass and the sun.

"Is anyone looking for us?" John asked furtively, looking out from under the brim of his cap.

"Just all the Meyers tribe and the Burditts, too," she said.

"Not the sheriff?"

"Well, the sheriff did help Father a little, John, but he had to spend most of his time looking for rebels—not runaways."

Jane missed the look of relief that passed between John and Nan.

"Land's sakes, Nan, I can see you're worn out," said Jane. "But you, John, what's that big grin on your face? We've been worried sick, and you come back like the cat who ate the robin. I told Mother not to worry, that the bad penny would show up soon! But I tell you, it's been no picnic around home. We've all been taking turns helping out."

"How are the folks?" John asked. "And how are George and Bleecker?"

"One question at a time. The folks are worn right out with worry over you both. Nan's mother's had a complete breakdown and hardly says a word. But Mr. Burditt, who has always been so quiet—well, he's talking plenty now. He keeps saying, 'If Nan comes home safe, I'll never complain about my wife talkin' so much again.' It's really pathetic to listen to him."

"I'm awful sorry," said John, though the only reason he saw to apologize was to stop Jane's ranting. It was affecting Nan badly. Her eyes were filling with tears.

"But where are George and Bleecker?" John asked again.

"Hold your horses, John! I'll get to them. Just listen.

Bleecker is home, thank goodness, since Hanna is expecting her baby any day now. But George was identified by a passenger as being on that steamer that was torched. So he's awaiting trial in Fort Henry along with a number of others."

Hmmm, that was good news and bad. The way things were going with him and Nan, it was better to have George away from home; still, someplace other than Fort Henry would have been nice. John didn't want anything really bad to happen to his brother.

"How are the folks managing?" he asked.

"As I was telling you, John," said Jane, "we married ones are all taking turns to help them out. And I haven't been feeling so well lately."

"Really? What's wrong with you? You were always as healthy as a horse."

"Thank you, John. I'm with child. And about time, too—I've been married six months. But I've been doing my share to help, just the same as the rest."

She waited expectantly, but John was darned if he was going to apolgize again. "Any news of Tobias?" he asked.

"He's being held in Kingston and will be tried at the July assizes, too. I can tell you, Father's been—"

Knock! Knock! The front door was rattling under the weight of a heavy fist. Jane stared at the runaways and said, "I wonder who that is? I wasn't expecting anyone." Then she hurried from the kitchen, through her hallway, and onto the front doorstep.

"Father! Thank goodness; you've come at just the right time. You'll never believe who's here. Nan and that runaway brother of mine!"

"Thank God." Jacob Meyers came rushing through the hallway behind his daughter.

"You gave us a terrible scare, John," he said. Then he looked over at Nan's tear-stained face. "We expected you back long ago. What on earth happened?"

John tried not to look too excited. The fewer folks who knew about his discovery the better. He would wait until he was alone with Father before he talked it over.

"Well, John?"

"We lost our way," John said quietly. "We just lost our way."

His father looked at his son's shining eyes and knew something was afoot. But this wasn't the time to discuss it. "We must get Nan home, at once. Her mother is nearly out of her mind with worry."

***

An hour later, Father steered the horses up the knoll between the trees into the Burditts' laneway and stopped the team at their neighbours' front door. Without a nod or a wave, Nan jumped down from the wagon, raced up to the house, flung open the front door, and disappeared inside.

"I'll hold the team," Father said. "You'd better see that every-thing's all right before we leave her. Her parents may not even be there."

John jumped lightly onto the ground and ran across the lawn and up the front steps two at a time. As he stepped inside, he met Nan already coming back from the kitchen. "No one's there," she said. She sailed past him and up the stairs.

John stood still at the foot of the stairs and listened as Nan opened amd shut the bedroom doors, shouting, "Ma, oh Ma, I'm home!"

"Nan?" came the sound of a feeble voice. He heard soft steps and Nan's voice saying, "Mother!"

Then, "Oh, Nan, you're safe. Oh, Nan, my poor dear child." Mrs. Burditt's voice, at first feeble and strained, gradually increased in strength and speed. "Why did you ever run away, Nan? You can't imagine what it's been like around here without you, my dear, dear child. I was just thinking about the day you first walked across the floor and said, 'Ma, Ma.' Did you know that, Nan, that the first words you ever did say were 'Ma, Ma'? It happened at the same time—the walking and talk-ing, and you were only eleven months old. You were the smartest baby around. Now, you must tell me about your trip. But first, I have to tell you that your Pa and I have been so worried about you, my dear, dear…"

John turned around and went out the front door. Mrs. Burditt seemed to be back to her normal self and Nan would be fine.

Back in the wagon, he looked up sideways at Father's set jawline. Jacob Meyers gave the horses a fast flick of the whip, and they were off down the Burditts' lane.

"Well, John," said Father, "start talking."

John didn't say a word. He just pulled one of the knapsacks up from the wagon floor and folded the leather back a little. In the narrow opening, the silver glinted in the sun's rays.

"The Silver Cave," Father breathed. He looked at John with unqualified admiration. "Close that bag, John, and don't say a word to anybody about this. Who else…?" Then he stopped and said, "Of course, Nan would know."

"She won't tell anyone. She got so mad at the time it took to dig this out, she said she never wants to hear another word about that Silver Cave again." It had been hard work taking the silver out with only a jacknife. They'd had to spend another two nights in the cave before they started making their way home. "But I did promise her a share."

"Of course, of course." Father looked excited and thoughtful at the same time. "If those two bags are filled with pure silver, there's a fortune there, John. But it will have to be taken to the

States to sell. And now is not the time to go south of the border. We'll have to wait. Right now, any of us could be accused of negotiating with the enemy and then searched if we planned such a trip."

"And of course there are *pirates* on the St. Lawrence," John smirked. He gave his father a sideways glance.

"What do you know about that?" asked Father, looking stern.

"I'd best not say. I'm not wanted for anything, am I?"

"Only for running away with a neighbour's girl. There may be a father over here with a shotgun. It's the talk of the neighbourhood."

John was shocked. "They don't think…"

"We didn't know what to think. But John Burditt's a reasonable man. He'll listen to his daughter's account first. I hope she gives a good account of your behaviour."

"She will," John said with confidence.

Just as they reached their laneway, they met a buggy coming down the opposite side of the road, pulled by a grey horse. Father drew his horses to a halt to let the buggy pass on before he turned in to his lane. But the small buggy with the black canopy came to a stop, directly opposite them. Miss Hildreth was driving, and she had a passenger: a lady whose face was shaded by a large, deep bonnet.

Father nodded. "Good day to you both. It's a fine day."

"Good day, Mr. Meyers," Miss Hildreth smiled. "Why, John, you're back!" Holding the horse's reins and staring across at him, she looked like any rosy-cheeked farm lass with her sparkling brown eyes and curly brown hair falling out loose across her forehead and flowing down her back from under her bonnet. "Are you all right? We missed you."

"I…uhh…just went on a little fishing trip after the seeding." John wondered why she'd missed him. He never went to school from April till mid-October. He was just too busy on the farm.

Then Miss Hildreth indicated her passenger. "I'd like you to meet Mother. She came up to visit me a few weeks back. She was caught in the middle of that awful raid on the *Sir Robert Peel.* Mother, this is John Meyers. He wasn't with the rest of the family that Sunday we dined with them."

John tried to look blank at the mention of the *Sir Robert Peel.* "Good day, madam," he said, taking off his cap. The older lady leaned forward to nod in greeting, and John felt himself blanch. She was the one who'd carried her carpetbag off the boat!

Fortunately, there was no glimmer of recognition in the woman's face as she said, "How do you do, young man? Are you one of Louise's pupils?"

"One of my oldest, Mother—why, you won't even be back in

the fall, will you, John? You completed all your assignments before you left in April. You'll be graduating with the Senior Fourth class."

That was right—he'd forgotten. John thought how strange it would be not to walk to school every weekday all winter long. He'd rather miss it—and Miss Hildreth, come to think of it. He'd warmed up to her considerably after the skating party. She had a girlish way of twisting a finger into one of the curls that fell on her cheek while she was reading. He used to watch with rapt attention when she pulled her finger from the ringlet and it snapped back into place again.

"How are you enjoying your visit, Mrs. Hildreth?" asked Father.

"Very much indeed, Mr. Meyers. But I'm waiting now to go back to New York with my daughter. It's only a week till the end of her term."

"Are you coming back in the fall, Miss Hildreth?" John asked politely. Then something else occured to him. Without school, there went his chance to see Nan every day. He'd have to ask Father for permission to court her officially, if George hadn't beaten him to it. His thoughts distracted him so, he didn't even hear Miss Hildreth's answer to his question.

Miss Hildreth flipped the reins lightly on her horse and the grey mare walked slowly onward. Mrs. Hildreth's words floated back to John clearly and distinctly: "I know I've met that boy before. His voice was so familiar."

Father stared over at John but did not catch his eye. John was too busy looking down.

23

John leaned against the iron fence that separated the Kington courthouse from the street. He was standing with his back to the crowd of people working their way inside. It was George's trial, and it seemed the whole countryside was there to watch. John had dropped off his father, mother, and brothers at the front of the impressive building and then gone to fasten the horses at a hitching post in the shed.

He really should be joining his family inside, but instead John was taking a few breaths of air out here. He gazed down the street, seeing nothing. He knew his family were all very worried about George, and John himself didn't want anything bad to happen to him. But a part of him held on to the knowledge that George's release meant the end of his own chances with Nan. It turned out that all those Sundays George had dressed up and gone out, he hadn't been going to Reformer meetings, as John had thought. He'd been visiting the Burditts. And Nan had sent word to George in jail that if he won his case, she would be waiting.

All this Nan had told him during a hasty stolen meeting two weeks ago. Nan had been forbidden to see or speak to any of the Meyers family after her wilderness escapade. It would make her promise to George difficult to keep, but she seemed keen on the challenge.

"Why didn't you say anything in the Silver Cave?" he had asked her miserably.

"Up to then, I thought you knew how I felt about George," she had said, eyes downcast. "And when you said...what you said, I was taken aback. I didn't want to hurt your feelings. You've always been like a brother to me, John. Better than that— a friend. I didn't want to spoil it."

And John had had to be content with that. Still, he thought it would be a long time before he would be able to pick up their friendship again.

John turned and stumbled ahead towards the big open doors. He didn't look about him at all the people. Everyone there knew the fate that might be in store for his brother, and he couldn't bear to see the curiousity and eagerness on their faces. To them, George was just another rebel, and if he went to the gallows they'd shake their heads in approval or dismay and then go about their business. But after today, the Meyers family might never be the same again.

He began to push through the crowd, saying, "Excuse me!" as he went. One person turned and said, "John!" It was his former teacher.

"Miss Hildreth!" he said. "What a surprise—to see you here, too! I guess the whole countryside has come. But I thought you'd be long gone for home."

"You can't get rid of me that fast, John Meyers!" She sounded friendly but she wasn't looking him in the eye. In fact, her brown eyes were fixed on the iron railing just behind John. And she was fidgeting a little with her hands in and out of her pockets. "I'm coming back to teach in the fall, you know."

"No, I didn't know," John said, "but I'm glad to hear it— even though I won't be in your class anymore. So, did your mother go back home without you, then?"

"Sort of…that is…my mother and I…we're still here. But we're going back home in a few days." She looked away from John again and was now examining the stone walkway. "I'm sorry, but I just have to go, John." She turned briskly, hurried through the wrought iron gate, and walked briskly down the street. She was soon lost from sight.

"What's wrong with her?" John wondered. She hadn't seemed like herself at all. Then he felt foolish. Who was he to know what was strange or normal about Miss Hildreth? And here he was talking to himself when he should be inside looking for his family.

It didn't take John long to find them, for Bleecker and Jake were waiting for him and they ushered him right up to the vacant spot on the polished oak bench at the front of the courtroom. Ahead of them, George sat in the prisoner's dock, along with Tobias and seven other prisoners. A few looked grimly down at their feet; others were staring at George or his lawyer, Mr. Macdonald. The man was tall, about the same height and age as George. His thick, black, wavy hair curled over his collar and out around his rather large ears. He was now bent over a wooden table just in front of the prisoner's dock, jotting down a few notes with a quill pen.

The court clerk rose and droned, "All rise for His Honour, Mr. Justice McLean." Everyone in the courtroom rose to his or her feet and the judge entered the room. "You may be seated," said the court clerk as he took his seat by the desk at the front of the room. The spectators, the jury, the prisoners, and the lawyers all sat down in unison.

While the preliminary statements were made, John studied the jury. He was happy to see a number of familiar faces, including many who would sympathize with George. They all looked hot in their suits and cravats. It was a sultry day in early July, and the breeze from the windows did not seem to be making its way very far into the room. John turned his attention back to the proceedings.

The Crown attorney, John S. Cartwright, was just calling his first witness to the stand—Anthony Post was his name. He was a short little man with straight brown hair, beady eyes, and bushy eyebrows. He seemed a little unbalanced as he swaggered forward, in flashy red boots, to the witness box between the judge and the jury. His gait, and the long red scarf that flowed out from his throat in two directions, gave him the appearance of a jaunty sailor. With his hand on the Bible, Anthony Post quietly promised to tell the truth, the whole truth, and nothing but the truth.

He looked like a strange rogue, John thought. And there was something familiar about the man. John stared at him a bit longer. That was it! The rogue was a sailor, or at least a pirate— one of those in the raid on the *Sir Robert Peel.* He had surely been bribed by someone from the Family Compact to identify George—and probably all the rest of them. John could see the prisoners shifting restlessly.

"Where were you on the night of May 29, in the year of our Lord 1838?" asked the Crown attorney in a quiet voice.

"I was on Wellesley Island, on the north shore of the eastern part of the island and south of the Bay—Lake of Isles."

"And what did you observe there?"

"First, I saw this Canadian steamship, the *Sir Robert Peel*, approaching the island."

"Where did she go?"

"She was on her way to Kingston. That's part of her regular route. She goes back and forth between the American and Canadian shores. She landed on the American side and the captain sent most of her crew over to gather firewood to refuel."

"Did there appear to be anything strange going on?"

"Not at that time, sir."

"When did you notice something unusual?"

A deeper silence fell over the courtroom.

"Well, an hour or so later, these farmers came out of the bush with their faces all painted."

"What did they do?"

"About a dozen men went on board the ship, while the rest prevented the crew from going back on to assist the passengers."

"And did you see *this* man?" The Crown attorney turned and pointed at George, the accused.

"Oh, yes, sir. He was right behind the leader, Pirate Bill."

A low murmur spread through the courtroom. "That will be all," said the attorney with a smug smile on his face. He took his seat.

The judge nodded to George's lawyer. "Do you have any questions for the witness, Mr. Macdonald?"

Mr. Macdonald leapt to his feet. "I do, Your Honour."

He turned to take up his note pad, and John remembered that long nose that matched his ears. John A. couldn't be a day over twenty-five, if that, John thought despairingly. How could such a young man possibly be able to do *anything* for George after that pirate had identified him so positively?

Mr. Macdonald approached the witness slowly and deliberately.

"I wonder why you were on that part of the Wellesley Island—on *American* soil—exactly at the place where a Canadian ship was about to stop. Do you work in that part of the island?"

"No, sir."

"Do you live anywhere on that island?"

"No, sir."

"Then perhaps you would like to tell us just why you were out 'strolling' at two o'clock in the morning on an island where you neither live nor work?"

"Objection, Your Honour!" shouted the Crown attorney. The older lawyer was standing on his feet now. "My client is not the man on trial here. He is not the one who has to account for *his* whereabouts."

"Objection overruled. May I remind you, Mr. Cartwright, of the procedure called 'cross-examination'? Proceed, Mr. Macdonald."

"So, how did you happen to be out strolling at that time of night?"

"Couldn't sleep, sir."

Mr. Macdonald raised his bushy eyebrows, turned to the audience, then swiftly turned back to the witness. "And where is your place of residence?"

"I'm a sailor. I've lived in many different places in the Thousand Islands."

"On the side of the American states or that of Upper Canada?"

"Both."

"Are you an American or a British subject, Mr. Post?"

"Sir, I am a loyal subject of Her Majesty Queen Victoria," Post answered, with a sanctimonious smirk.

"What did you see," said John A., "when you just happened to be out strolling on the *north* shore of the island at one or two o'clock on the morning of the thirtieth of May, in the year of our Lord 1838?"

"I saw the steamship—*and* that fellow over there leading a group of raiders onto it."

"Let the record show that the witness pointed to Mr. George Meyers," the judge commented to the clerk.

Macdonald went on. "You said that the men's faces were painted?"

"Yes, sir."

"But the one you recognized was not painted, is that it? The one you recognized was making no attempt to disguise himself?"

"Oh, no, sir. He was up to no good. He was even more painted than the others!"

"Did you recognize any of the others?"

"No, sir, I'm afraid not."

There were sighs of relief from the other prisoners seated just behind George in the prisoner's dock.

"But you say you recognized Mr Meyers even though he was 'even more painted than the others.' How interesting."

"Yes, sir."

"Also, wasn't it very dark throughout most of the night?"

"Yes, sir, it was. But there were times when the clouds lifted and the moon shone through. It only takes one glimpse, sir, to see a face and never forget it."

John A. rubbed his clean-shaven chin and looked down at the witness. "Had you ever seen George Meyers before that night?"

"Oh, no, sir. He was no acquaintance of mine."

"Yet you have identified him—a man you had never seen before and who, you admit, was even more disguised than others whom you *cannot* identify!" John A. rolled his eyes upward and shook his head, then he shot a fast glance at the jury and said,

"That's all, Your Honour."

"You may take your seat," said the judge to the witness, and low voices buzzed around the courtroom. "Silence!" ordered the judge, thumping his gavel on the desk. "Call the next witness," he said.

John gasped. The witness was Nan's father, John Burditt. Why was he a witness for the *Crown?* Was John Burditt so angry about his daughter's disappearance that he was ready to send any Meyers boy to the gallows? It seemed a terrible retribution.

The witness was sworn in and the questioning began.

"Where do you live?" asked the Crown.

"In Sydney Township, on the farm next to Jacob Meyers."

"Do you remember seeing George at home any time during the week of May 29?"

"Yes, I believe I did, but I couldn't swear to it. It wouldn't be unusual if I hadn't seen him that week. Farmers work hard to earn a living. We don't rightly have the time always to keep track of our own children, let alone our neighbours."

There were titters of laughter around the courtroom. It was all over the township that Nan Burditt and John Meyers had run away together and then decided to come back home.

"You're not sure, then, that George was at home?"

"No, I can't say I didn't see him and I can't say I did. I was busy with my own affairs. And I don't go spying on my neighbours."

"Last December, there was a rebellion in Toronto. Was it also a fact that George was in Toronto during that whole time—and in fact, for a number of days afterwards?"

John A. leaped to his feet. "Objection, Your Honour! Past events have no bearing on the present case."

"Let the witness answer, but do not persist in this line of questioning any longer, Mr. Cartwright."

"Once again, sir, I do not have the time to keep track of my neighbours. But I do know that George was at home in December last year for his sister's wedding. I was one of the guests. You can also check this fact with Bishop Strachan of the Church of England, who performed the nuptials, and who is a friend of the family."

"That's all, Your Honour," said the lawyer. He sat down speedily. Any mention of the family's connection to Bishop Strachan would only help the defendant.

"Any cross-examination?" asked the judge.

John A. nodded, got up slowly, and approached the witness. "You say that you are a neighbour of Jacob Meyers."

"Yes, sir, for these past many years."

"What kind of neighbour is he?"

"A family you can rely on. He and his wife and the boys will always help a neighbour in need. We share the work on our farms sometimes. But we're independent, too. Each farming family shares and helps the other, but we all lead independent lives, don't check on one another's business. Jacob Meyers is a hard-working, honest man who has raised four sons and three daughters to be the same."

"Then is it your opinion that his son George could not have been involved in this reckless attack on our Canadian steamer, the *Sir Robert Peel?*"

"Yes, it is my *opinion* that he was not involved."

The Crown attorney was on his feet and shouting, "I object! Opinions are not admissible! We want facts!"

"Objection sustained. Mr. Macdonald, keep to the facts."

"Thank you, Mr. Burditt, you may be seated," said Macdonald. John heaved a sigh of relief as Nan's father headed for his seat.

"Bring in the next witness," said the judge.

Now, John's heart sank to his boots. In walked the schoolteacher's mother, Mrs. Hildreth. Now he knew why Miss Hildreth was still around. Now he knew the reason for her strange behaviour when he'd bumped into her just outside the courthouse. She hadn't even looked him straight in the face. It was all clear to him. Her mother was going to testify against George!

Mrs. Hildreth held her head high and sedately approached the front. Her straight bodice and pleated sleeves were the latest style and added an elegance that made the audience aware that the lady had come from a larger, more stylish city. John lowered his head. Poor George! This woman had been there and was one of the innocent victims! John kept his head down as she entered the stand.

After the sworn oath, the Crown began. "Please identify yourself."

"I am Mrs. William Hildreth of New York City, and I was a passenger on the *Sir Robert Peel* on that *terrible* night of May 29."

"Where were you headed?"

"To Kingston and then on to Sydney Township."

"Why were you travelling to Sydney Township?"

"My daughter is a teacher there. I was going to visit her until the end of the term and intended to accompany her back home."

"Were you treated badly by the prisoners?"

"Yes, I was made to disembark the ship in my night attire! I did not take kindly to that!"

"Did anyone attack your person?"

"Only my carpetbag of belongings."

"What happened?"

"A very rude invader grabbed it from me. I shouted at him.

Then a younger man grabbed my bag from the rude one and returned it to me."

"How do you know the second man was younger?"

"By his voice. I train a choir at home. The boy's voice had changed, but I could recognize that it was a younger voice."

"Did anyone else assail you?"

"No."

"What did the boy call out to the man who took your carpetbag?"

"He said that 'George' had ordered them not to hurt anyone."

John could feel the eyes of his family trying not to look at him. To his horror, he blushed to the roots of his hair. He glanced at the jury—a few of the Belleville men were looking at him. He slunk down in his seat.

"No further questions, Your Honour." The Crown attorney again smugly took his seat.

John A. was striding up to the witness stand. He began.

"Many men in the British colonies were named George— after George III, the reigning English monarch during the time of the American Revolution. And the name has come down through Loyalist families. Such is the case with the defendant, whose grandfather was John W. Meyers, a Loyalist and a spy for the British. This grandfather named his eldest son George. Then

John Meyers' youngest son, Jacob, the father of the accused, named this son George. It has become a family name."

John didn't know if Mrs. Hildreth cared about all this, but suspected it was all for the jury's benefit anyway—and the judge's. And why not? After all, they were the most important here. The jury would declare George's innocence or guilt, and if the latter, the judge would sentence his brother. It was a wise approach.

The woman stared stoically at the young lawyer as he continued. "So, since there are many Georges in Upper Canada, this does not mean that the George referred to on board the *Sir Robert Peel* is, in fact, *this* George. Do you agree?"

A hushed silence fell across the audience.

"I suppose," came the crisp words of the witness. She did not appear to be the least bit flustered.

"You say the night was very dark," Mr. Macdonald continued, "and you could only identify the man who defended you as being younger *because of his voice*. So, would you be able to recognize him on sight?"

"I doubt that. All the men's faces were painted!"

"Look around the courtroom. Many of George's friends are here. The young man you have been referring to might well be here."

Whose side is he on?! thought John. The woman's eyes travelled slowly over the courtroom. John sank even lower into his seat and stared at his feet. But he couldn't help it. He had to look up.

The woman's eyes were upon him. The corners of her mouth twitched a little as though she was about to smile. John felt his face flush again, as red as his hair. He felt as if those eyes were drilling a hole through his head.

"I don't recognize anyone," she said at last.

"Do you recognize the prisoner?"

There was a long silence in the courtroom again as she turned to look at George. No one in the audience seemed to be breathing.

"Let the accused rise, so that the witness may see you more clearly," the judge said crisply.

George rose slowly. His dark brown hair and clear blue eyes were a sharp contrast to the pallor of his skin as he turned and faced the woman directly.

The silence in the courtroom was shattering. John felt his muscles tighten.

At last, she opened her mouth to speak. "No, sir, I do not recognize the prisoner," she said crisply. "I do not think I ever saw this man in my life before."

John's breath came back in short gasps. He could hear sighs of relief all around him.

"Counsel, would you like to re-examine?" the judge asked.

"No, Your Honour," the Crown attorney replied. "The Crown rests its case."

After Mrs. Hildreth stepped down from the witness stand, it was Mr. Macdonald's turn. He brought forward a half-dozen character witnesses for George and the whole Meyers family: neighbouring farmers, Belleville church friends, and the like. John began to sit up straight again as one witness after another spoke his piece. He hadn't known the Meyerses were such models of propriety and virtue. The Crown tried to make the witnesses contradict themselves, and one other, but they stuck stubbornly to their statements.

"We shall adjourn for the day," said the judge when the questioning was concluded. "Tomorrow, Saturday, the seventh of July, we will gather to hear the lawyers' closing remarks to the jury before they are closeted to make their decision."

As the judge's long robes disappeared around the corner of the doorway leading to his chambers, George turned to look once more on his father and brothers. When he got to John, he nodded and smiled kindly. Then he was led from the room.

24

The jury was out for two days solid. The Meyers family ate and drank and talked during that time, but stiffly and without animation. Everyone and everything seemed to John to be holding its breath. On Monday afternoon they were called back to the court. The room was packed even more than before, for word had spread. Yet the crowd was completely silent.

John stared at his brother's stiff back and a large lump rose in his throat. The foreman of the jury walked up to the judge's desk and handed him a paper. The judge unfolded it, read it silently, and then returned it to the man.

By now the atmosphere was so intense that John felt as if he was about to suffocate. Then the foreman turned and faced the courtroom filled with farmers, George's friends, Kingston townspeople, reporters from the Kingston *Chronicle and Gazette*, and the other prisoners.

"Let the foreman give the verdict," intoned the judge.

"Not guilty, Your Honour!"

His words rang in the ensuing silence like music. There was a spontaneous burst of applause, then the stampede began as neighbours and friends piled out of their places and rushed down the narrow aisles to reach George with handshakes, hugs, and slaps on the back.

The judge's gavel hit the desk. Everyone stopped in their tracks. "Please be seated," he boomed out.

Without a murmur, everyone slipped back into their seats and stared up at the judge.

"In light of this decision," the judge pronounced, "I conclude that there is no need to hold any of the remaining eight prisoners also suspected in this raid."

Applause erupted once more, dying down only when the audience noticed that the judge had more to say.

"The evidence for the others accused hangs on the testimony given by this principal witness. Since the case against George Meyers was the strongest, yet could not be proved, it would be a waste of the public purse to carry on any further. The charges against the other eight prisoners being held under the same suspicion are now dismissed." He looked directly at the prisoners in the front row. "You are free to go home."

This time a blast of cheers filled the courtroom, and loud, steady clapping followed the old judge as he hurried from the room. Family and friends rushed to the front to hug their delin-quent sons. Mother was among the first—seeking out Tobias, who was grinning from ear to ear.

John clapped his older brother on the shoulder. "Well, George," he said, "your second reprieve! And it's a good thing, too. We need you for the harvest. There's going to be a bumper crop of wheat in August." George smiled, his blue eyes twinkling, but his pallor remained and he had no quick retort. This adven-ture must have shaken him up, thought John.

John walked out of the courthouse while Father made the arrangements to pick up George and Tobias. He leaned against the iron fence that separated the courthouse from the street and took a few breaths of the fresh air. He was supposed to fetch the horses, but he thought he'd wait until his parents appeared. Then he spotted Miss Hildreth, her mother not far behind. He remembered the strange look she'd given him during her testi-mony and turned toward the shed. Too late!

"John!" Miss Hildreth shouted and pushed through the crowd. Her cheeks were rosy and her dark hair shone. Well, her mother might be a bit of a battle-axe, but Miss Hildreth was cer-tainly easy on the eyes.

"I'm so glad George and Tobias are free," she said, looking directly at John with her big brown eyes. All the awkwardness of their past conversation was gone.

"Really!" said John, breaking into a big freckled grin. "I'm glad you're coming back to teach school this September."

"I'm looking forward to it," she said, her dark brown eyes shining up at him. "I like Sydney Township. It's a beautiful place to live and the folks there have all been so good to me. I'm glad they want me back."

"What are your plans for the summer, Miss Hildreth?" John asked. He was remembering the older man from Belleville, who had escorted her to the skating party way back in February.

"Please, just call me Louise," she said. "I'm not your teacher any longer." She hesitated while John took in her words. "Oh…I plan to swim and sail and just relax. We have a cottage on Long Island. What about you, John? What will you do all summer?"

"Well…Louise," said John. Looking down at her this way, he didn't feel at all out of place using the name. But then he saw Mrs. Hildreth sailing up behind, and he started to stammer.

"I…I guess I'll have to work hard all summer…on the farm, that is. Any farm's a busy place in the summer." Now he felt like a bumbling cowhand again.

Mrs. Hildreth gave John a cold nod and said to her daughter, "We must be on our way. I certainly don't want to miss the boat."

Louise ignored her mother and went on, "Well, John, if you ever come to New York, be sure to visit us. At home or on Long Island. We'd be pleased to see you."

Suddenly, John thought about the silver. He had to go to the States sometime, to get rid of it. And the sooner the better. It made him nervous having all that wealth around.

"I'd love to," he said. "Sometimes there's a lull in the farmwork in early August. I'll let you know."

"Even the boat trip is enjoyable," Louise said.

"When there aren't any pirates," Mrs. Hildreth added looking straight at John. "We'll be sleeping in our daytime attire on this voyage, just in case. Come along, Louise." Mrs. Hildreth walked on ahead. John's face burned.

Louise hurried on to catch up with her mother, but she called back, "I'll write!" She waved gaily over her shoulder.

John waved back until the two women disappeared in the crowd. Then he strode over to the shed feeling not quite so unhappy about Nan. In fact, he was starting to feel good again. George was free, he had pounds of silver in his possession, and Louise Hildreth seemed to really like him. He was sure of that. A fellow had a feeling about these things.

He whistled as he brought out the horses. With or without the silver, he was going to visit Louise in August. Tobias owed him a few chores!

**

An hour later, George had collected his belongings from the jail that had been his home for the past six weeks, and the much-relieved Meyers family were finally on their way home. John was driving, with Mother on one side of him and Father and George on the other. It was good to be back out in the open air, with the evening breeze tousling his still, regrettably, very red hair.

Bleecker, Jake, and Tobias had taken Bleecker's light carriage and were planning to drive nonstop until they got to the Meyers farm. But even in the farm wagon, John expected to make good time. It was a long ride from Kingston to Sydenham Township—just over sixty miles; but with hardly any load, the horses could make four miles to the hour. They'd reach Bath late that night and stay at the inn there.

"Now, George," Father began after they were well away and past the sights of Kingston. "I hope your courtroom success hasn't gone to your head. I'd like you to know that you've put your mother and me through pure agony. We expect to see the end of all this rebellion business, as far as you're concerned...."

Father's thundering voice was growing louder. Here it comes, thought John. George may have been exonerated in the courtroom, but at home with Father there was no escaping justice. He was Crown, jury, and judge all rolled in one.

Then Mother spoke out, almost for the first time that day. "Jacob," she said calmly, "I've had enough. I think George's six weeks in jail were enough punishment. The farm is waiting, and there's lots of work to be done. Let's just all try to get back to normal. Shall we?"

Father turned to Mother, and John saw his shoulders lower and his set neck relax. "Yes, Jane," he said.

Well, well, thought John, and he silently thanked God for Mother. They rode on in silence, and in a little while, John went back to dreaming about his farm, and the house he would build for the girl of his dreams—whose hair, somehow, had changed from straight brown locks to long dark curls. The house would be built from the proceeds of silver he personally had mined! What an adventure that had been! He'd really enjoyed every minute of it. Of course, he was still planning to share the treasure with Nan—good sport that she was. He really felt quite affectionate about her, after all.

"Hey, Johnny!" George shouted. "Watch out!"

John looked, and, sure enough, there was a whole bag of grain, dropped by some farmer, right in the middle of the road. John yanked on the reins and steered the two horses around it.

"What *are* you doing, John?" said Mother, who'd been roused from a catnap.

"Trying to dump us all in the lake, that's what!" said George.

"Don't you think it's my turn to drive, little brother?"

"No, George, you take it easy. Last time I let you drive, we didn't get back for a long, long time."

Father chuckled and Mother put her head back on his shoulder.

"I can't say much to that, now, can I?" said George, grinning up at his red-haired brother.

John grinned back at him. "No, George, you can't, but that's never stopped you before!"

"You're right, not much stops me...or you, either, Johnny." George punched John gently on the arm and settled back in the wagon.

John gave the reins a gentle flick, and Bonnie and Duke got back to their former speed. It was going to be good to have George home again. After all, he was his brother, and the Meyers family always stuck together—no matter what.

HISTORICAL NOTE

As in all works of historical fiction, most of the characters and events in this novel are real—but they have been blended and rearranged to make a better story. John was a real person and so were all the members of his family, as well as Nancy (Nan) Burditt and Louise Hildreth. John's brothers Tobias, Bleecker, and George really were involved in the Upper Canada Rebellion—but John was not.

To simplify the story, I gave all of Tobias's and Bleecker's actions to George. However, Tobias W. Meyers was taken prisoner, on February 24, 1838, and was kept at Fort Henry until July 9, 1838. Dr. Bleecker W. Meyers was imprisoned for eighty-two days at Fort Henry in Kingston in 1838, then discharged without a trial. Jacob's sons were among more than eighty Midland District men arrested and jailed for a time in the first half of 1838 under suspicion of helping the rebel cause. The Midland men around the Belleville area were, in fact, the men who scuttled the *Sir Robert Peel*, and the Belleville militia did meet them at Napanee on the way back. Jacob Meyers had served as a captain in the militia, and it was likely that he would have been called upon again in 1838—though not necessarily to arrest his own sons!

George's activities appear to be centred in Toronto, where he truly was caught delivering papers to Mackenzie's house, according to records in the Archives of Ontario. It appears that he participated in battle there, as well. On the other hand, there is no evidence that George was involved in the burning of the *Sir Robert Peel*.

For some reason, Bleecker was released before the trial in Kingston. At the actual trial, the person actually accused and freed was a man by the name of William Anderson. The others involved, including Tobias, were subsequently freed without a trial. And it is true that John A. Macdonald, who later became the first prime minister of Canada and was eventually knighted, was the defence lawyer for the case. At that time he was a young hotshot lawyer, described thus in the July 11, 1838, edition of the *Kingston Chronicle and Gazette*: "J.A. Macdonald, who, though one of the youngest barristers in the Province, is rapidly rising in his profession."

William Lyon Mackenzie was elected mayor of Toronto in 1835. The humorous anecdote about Yonge Street mud credited to him in this book was related in *The Firebrand* by William Kilbourn, an excellent resource that also inspired Mackenzie's speeches as they appear in

Meyers' Rebellion. And Pirate Bill Johnston did exist—and with an American price on his head. He was captured and sentenced to one year in jail at Albany, New York. He escaped after six months and went into hiding in the Thousand Islands. In 1841, U.S. President William Henry Harrison pardoned him.

Any Canadians who were found guilty of treason were either hanged—as Samuel Lount and Peter Matthews were—or banished to "Van Diemen's Land" (Australia). At the time of the Rebellion, ninety-two prisoners were transported there from Upper Canada. Thirteen died shortly upon arrival; less than half returned when amnesty was declared for the Upper Canada rebels in 1849. At this time, Mackenzie and many other rebels who had fled to the United States also returned to Canada. In 1851, Mackenzie won the seat for Haldimand County in the Legislative Assembly of Canada. Unable to regain a leadership position, he retired to private life in 1858. His daughter Isabel, who was born while the family was in exile in the United States, was to be the mother of the Right Honourable William Lyon Mackenzie King, prime minister of Canada from 1921 to 1925, 1926 to 1930, and 1936 to 1948.

In 1845, all three of the Meyers men made claims for damages and monies lost due to what they claimed was their "unjust imprisonment." Their claims of losses, on file at the Archives of Ontario, are as follows: Tobias, 139 pounds; Bleecker, 50 pounds; and George, 332 pounds. It is interesting to note that their requests far exceed the modest amounts (four pounds, or ten or fourteen, for instance) claimed by their contemporaries. Even more notable is the fact that they were not awarded a single cent, though many others were given small amounts of compensation. (This may suggest that their actual guilt was known.) In contrast, their father, Jacob Meyers, was given compensation for the British military's use of his grounds, his outbuildings, and his firewood while the soldiers were billeted at his home.

John did not participate in the rebel activities of his older brothers, and if you wish to know whom the two youngest boys of the Meyers family *did* marry, you will need to consult the marriage records in Belleville—or wait for a sequel to this book.

Many historians view the Canadian rebellions of the mid–nineteenth century as failures. Though it is true that the rebels of Upper and Lower Canada won none of the battles that took place from the 1830s to the 1850s, they were a vital part of the establishment of strong democratic principles in Canada. The battles were a wake-up call for the British government, which responded first by replacing

Lieutenant-Governor Sir Francis Bond Head with Sir George Arthur, then by sending in Lord Durham, who arrived at Quebec City in late May, 1838. He was the author of an influential report which recommended that the two Canadas, Upper and Lower, be united under one legislature, and that the new entity be awarded government with members of parliament elected by, and responsible to, the people.

The process of change was not peaceful. It brought about loss of life, great personal sacrifice, and permanent banishment for some; yet it never erupted into a full-fledged revolution. Perhaps if more blood had been shed and large-scale war had broken out, the rebels would have gone down in history as great visionaries and leaders. As events played out, however, they have been given a place of relative obscurity, even though their actions prevented a Canadian aristocracy from taking root and helped establish the foundations of peace, order, and good government on which Canada's political structures are now based.

As for the Silver Cave, Native people were known to have come to Belleville from the north, carrying silver with them. But they would never reveal where it had come from. "The Silver Cave" has long been part of stories passed down through the generations in my family. I am a descendant of John's Grandpa Meyers. He was certainly convinced of the existence of the cave, and he truly did travel in November with a Native friend to find it. While theories differ as to how it came about, it is a generally accepted fact that Meyers lost his life from pneumonia after he caught a terrible chill on that trip. And Jacob's oldest son, John—not the John who is the hero of this novel—is said to have lost his life because of injuries he suffered on the same quest.

There is a very small settlement not far south of beautiful Bon Echo Provincial Park called Myers Cave—and no one living there knows how it got its name. Within the park, a sheer cliff rises three hundred feet out of the clear blue waters of Lake Mazinaw. On that rock face are over two hundred original Native paintings. From these depictions, we know the Natives thought this spot important; perhaps some of those markings describe the silver cave. Still, the location of the cave remains a mystery.

Robert Bruce, a retired OPP officer and one of my relatives, has scoured the terrain in detail, and farmers and other property owners in the area have searched their land for signs of the cave, all without success. I strongly recommend, however, that no one search without proper equipment, supplies, skills—and a competent adult. Anyone could easily get lost and perish in that wilderness. There is still a great deal of unsold Crown land in the area, with no roads to make it accessible. Even where there are roads, the boulders are so large, the bush so thick, and the underbrush so deep that anyone lost there might never be found.

Perhaps someday, however, a stone behind a willow tree will be rolled back to reveal a small crevice opening into a real silver cave. Then Meyers' Cave will finally be found—probably by someone who is no descendant of the Meyers family, but who, perhaps, has travelled to the spot from a foreign land to look at this beautiful sight and who, like Grandpa Meyers did so long ago, might stay to make Canada home.